The Rising Star's Fake Girlfriend

Sweet Country Music Romance Book 1

Penelope Spark

1

She's the most beautiful woman I've ever seen. Cole was certain he could stay lost in those deep, dark eyes forever. She was the one. He could feel it. He reached across the table and put his hand over hers, and he smiled so broadly he feared his face might crack. He knew he probably looked like a fool, but he didn't care. He'd be a fool for love any day. He opened his mouth to declare his devotion but then paused with his mouth hanging open. Why was the waitress coming at him like a runaway Peterbilt?

She looked like a lunatic, wild hair sticking out in every direction in multiple shades of pink, her eyes so focused they appeared to be trying to drill holes into his face. There was no doubt she was coming for him, but he couldn't imagine why. Some part of his brain told him to look around him. Surely she had to be coming for someone else nearby. But he couldn't tear his eyes away from her, in part for fear that she would kill him while his eyes were averted. She certainly looked murderous. Her lips started moving as she drew nearer to them, and he felt as though everything was moving in slow motion. What did this woman want with him?

"What?" he managed. He couldn't make out her words. Even though she was still a dozen feet away, she was whispering. She was also closing the gap—fast.

His date turned to look, but before she could even get her head turned, the waitress was on them.

Her wide smile came off as part desperate, part sinister, as she leaned toward him. "Go to the bathroom, now!" She was still whispering. Sort of. She sounded as though she'd been in a life raft screaming for help and had lost her voice but was continuing to holler for the Coast Guard.

He didn't think he'd ever heard anyone sound so desperate. "What?" he asked again, and looked to his date for help, but the waitress put both hands on the table and leaned toward him, effectively blocking his date from his view.

"Now!" she whisper-cried again, her eyes wide and wild.

Somewhat against his will, he made eye contact with her. And froze. There was something about those eyes. Something startlingly sincere.

"Are you nuts?" she whispered, her mouth only inches from his face. "Bathroom! You're out of time!"

I don't think I'm *the one who's nuts here, ma'am.* He tried to glance apologetically at his date, but he couldn't see her. So he went to the bathroom. What else could he do? *When a crazy waitress tells me to go to the bathroom, I go, right?*

She followed him so closely on his heels, her presence made him move faster. He felt something akin to fear as he entered the dimly lit hallway that led to the bathrooms. She grabbed him by the arm, from behind.

He turned to face her. "What?" he said for the third time.

Her face had relaxed. A little. "Didn't mean to scare you, but you were almost just busted."

"What?" It occurred to him that he was demonstrating a limited vocabulary. He vowed to use a different word next time.

She let go of his arm and folded hers across her chest. "There's a large window in the bathroom. I would use it if I were you. Or stay in there for a very long time and then come out and just leave." She glanced over her shoulder. "I have to go. I don't have time to explain, but the woman you're making googly eyes at is married, and you were just about to get caught."

His head spun. He reached behind him for the wall, which, he was grateful, was there for him, and he leaned against it. *What* had she just said? That wasn't possible. Natalie wasn't married. He'd been seeing her for *weeks*. Surely he would've seen the signs if she was married.

The pink-haired waitress whirled away. "You're welcome," she said without looking at him.

He opened his mouth to say something, but nothing came out. So, after several long seconds in the dingy hallway, he went into the bathroom. Because that's what he'd been told to do. On some level, he knew this was absurd. But his brain wasn't functioning at full capacity. All he could think about was Natalie. He took out his phone and texted her, "Is it true?" Then he stared blankly at his phone, willing it to notify him of her response.

It didn't. Her phone was probably on silent. She'd been on a date, after all.

It occurred to him that Natalie might not understand what he'd meant. So, he texted, "The waitress says you're married. That's crazy, right?" Send.

Still nothing. He couldn't believe he was texting her from the bathroom when she was only thirty feet away. Oh, how his heart ached for her. Yet, he was furious. With the waitress if it wasn't true. With Natalie if it *was* true. But mostly with himself. How could he be that stupid?

But he wasn't that stupid. She wasn't married. Impossible. He felt defensive of her then. Why was he taking some crazy waitress's word for it? This was all some big misunderstanding. He looked at the giant window. Yep, that *was* big enough to climb through, but he had no intention of doing something so ridiculous.

He washed his hands out of habit, checked his silent phone one more time before sliding it back into his pocket, and then returned to the dining room. He would go back to his seat and ask Natalie to tell him the truth, and then they would have a good laugh.

Except Natalie was gone. Miss Pink Hair was behind the bar, leaning on it, talking to some mangy-looking fella with greasy hair.

"Lettie," another waitress called to her. "Table three is asking for refills."

Miss Pink Hair nodded toward her, then looked at him, and her eyes grew wide. She seemed surprised that he hadn't obeyed her escape order. He headed toward her, to ask her where his date had gone. Had she told Natalie to climb out the window in the ladies' room? If so, maybe he should have followed her instructions. Then he and Natalie could have met on the outside.

The waitress subtly shook her head and slid her eyes to the mangy guy. She was trying to telepathically communicate something, but what? The mangy guy looked at him, and his eyes grew wide with excitement. This wasn't alarming, though. This happened all the time with Cole. He was a rising star, after all. On some level, he knew he should give heed to her warning, but he was already moving, and the mangy man was staring at him. So he slid onto a bar stool and acted as though that had been his intent all along.

Miss Pink Hair, who also apparently went by the name of Lettie, turned and grabbed a whiskey bottle, presumably for table three, as Mr. Mange approached him.

"Cole Washburne! What an honor to meet you!" He stuck out his hand.

Cole took it and tried to hide his grimace at how damp it was.

"I'm a big fan! Almost didn't recognize you without your cowboy hat."

Shoot. He'd left his hat hanging on the coat rack by the booth he'd been sitting in. He resisted the urge to turn and look at it to make sure it was still there. He was suddenly desperate for it, but something told him not to let this guy know that. Cole smiled, unsure of what to say. After an awkward hesitation, he went with, "I appreciate that."

"The name's Darren."

Cole nodded. "It's a pleasure." Except that it wasn't, and Cole knew that he wasn't a very good liar. He hoped he sounded more convincing to Darren than he did to himself. He found himself longing for Lettie, hoping she'd interfere. And where on earth had Natalie gone? And he wanted his hat, dang it.

"What brings you here?" Darren asked, and there was an edge to his voice.

Cole searched for words. "Uh ... just trying to relax, I guess."

"Oh yeah? You weren't here because of Natalie, were you?"

He tried to look perplexed. "Who?"

Darren smirked. "I'm surprised to see you here is all. This place isn't really popular with people like you."

Cole raised an eyebrow. *People like me?*

2

Lettie watched the interaction. Could that cowpoke be any stupider? She'd tried to save him, gone out of her way to help, and then there he sat, a glutton for punishment. She was surprised that she'd had the urge to save him at all, surprised even more so that she still had the urge. She should just let him go down with the ship. He'd been foolish enough to be out in public holding hands with a married woman. Let him get what he had coming to him.

Except that she couldn't. Grudgingly, she approached.

"Can I get you anything?" she asked, leaning on the counter and forcing a smile at Cole.

"No, thank you, honey." He reached out and put his hand over hers and squeezed.

It took all of her will not to yank it away. What was he doing?

"I just came to see you."

Darren barked out a laugh. "What?"

Cole flashed him a smile far too wide to be sincere. "Yeah, this here's my girl."

Still laughing, Darren said, "Oh, she is, is she? That's funny. I've never heard her mention you."

Cole's face fell.

Oh my word, he's the worst liar in the world. He really didn't know she was married. He could never pull off an extramarital affair.

"No ... it's true," she stammered and leaned closer to him. As she did, she caught a whiff of him. He smelled like cedar, and something inside her warmed at that. She tried to ignore that feeling, though, and focus on the crisis at hand. "We've only just started seeing each other, and ..." She looked at Cole for help.

He offered none.

"And ..." She returned her eyes to Darren. "Obviously, I wouldn't tell you about it, because it's just so ... strange." *Oh wow, I am really struggling here.* Then she had an idea. Diversion is the illusionist's friend. "But never mind us. I just saw your girl walk by outside."

Darren's head jerked around like a hound who'd caught a scent on the wind. "Which way?"

"Going east."

Darren nearly flew out the door.

She promptly shook Cole's hand off hers. "Are you nuts?"

He let out a big puff of air and stood. "You sure you saw her going east?" He turned toward the booth he'd been sitting at, and she realized his hat was still hanging over his seat.

"No, you imbecile. Sit down! He'll probably be back in seconds."

He stopped walking and turned halfway around as if he couldn't decide which direction to go.

She hurried around the bar and toward the booth. "I just said that to get rid of him." She grabbed his hat and returned to him, holding it out to him without getting too close. Part of her wanted to smell the cedar again, and the rest of her was screaming that smelling him again was a bad idea.

He took a step closer to her, and the scent washed over her. She managed to ignore it, but it wasn't easy. She never should've started this. She should have just let him get caught. He took his hat. "Much obliged," he said, and she rolled her eyes. He was too wholesome to even be real, and yet, she knew that he was.

"You're welcome," she said, surprised at how soft her own voice sounded. "Now, get out of here." She tried to slide by him, but he grabbed her arm.

"Who was that guy?" Cole's eyes flicked to the doorway, and she knew without looking that Darren was back. Cole leaned toward her ear, and she felt the warmth of his breath on her neck. "How did he know I was with Natalie?"

She looked up at him. "He's a private investigator." She spoke so quietly that she barely made a sound.

But it was obvious that Cole heard her. His eyes slowly fell shut, as if he'd just received terrible news he couldn't quite process. "So it's true."

"What's true?" Darren asked.

Lettie's heart cracked for this silly cowboy. She slid her arm around Mr. Cedar's waist and said, "Nothing. Why are you back?"

Darren's eyes flicked back and forth between them.

She was so annoyed with him right now. Couldn't he just let this thing go?

"I didn't see her anywhere. Are you sure you saw her?" His eyes narrowed at Lettie.

"Nope. Not sure about anything except that I'm on the clock, so you both"—she looked up into Cole's eyes—"need to get out of here."

"Okay, Lettie, you can drop the act. I know you two aren't really dating."

That was it. She'd had enough. She let her arm drop from Cole's incredibly tight waist and said, "Enough!"

Darren's head jerked back at her volume, or maybe it was her pitch.

"I don't have to explain myself to you. I never have had to! I feel oh so bad that you didn't catch her doing anything wrong. Maybe she was just here for a drink! But she's not here now, so get out and leave us alone!"

Darren backed up a few steps without turning around. He stared at Cole for several seconds and then looked back at her. But then something shifted in his expression, and he took two quick steps toward them, so he was right in her face. "I know you are full of it. I know he was here with her. What I don't know is why you're covering for him."

She stared back at him, not knowing what to say. She was about to give up the whole ruse, when out of nowhere, Cole grabbed her, spun her toward him, and dipped her as if they had just been pronounced man and wife. Her stomach flipped as if she was on a roller coaster, and before she could even process what was happening, his lips were on hers. She started to jerk her head back, but then she couldn't. His lips were oh so warm, and it felt as though they were massaging hers. It felt *good*, and even though he was just a silly cowboy, she didn't want it to stop. But then it did. He returned her to her former upright position, and she was so dizzy she had to step back to keep from falling over. She put the back of her hand to her lips as if to trap the tingling that remained there.

"There," Cole said, his voice sounding huskier than it had a minute ago. "I don't kiss strangers like that. I don't know who you are, or who this Natalie woman is, or what your problem is, but I've reported fans for harassment before, and I'll do it again if I need to." He pointed to the door. "I believe Lettie asked you to leave."

Darren rolled his lips together, looking contemplative. Then he nodded and turned to go. Lettie watched him leave, feeling immensely grateful at his absence. When the door swung shut behind him, she turned to look up at Cole.

"Sorry, I shouldn't have kissed you like that without permission. I just really can't have anyone finding out I was involved with a ... a ... you know."

"No big deal," she said, even though the kiss had *felt* a little like a big deal.

He averted her gaze. "I appreciate your help." And then he was out the door before she could say another word.

3

Cole stepped out into the afternoon sunlight, took a few steps toward his truck, and then stopped. He felt sick to his stomach. Natalie ... married? He couldn't believe it. He didn't want to believe it. He'd been so sure she was the one, and she'd been lying to him. He pinched his eyes shut. How could he have been so stupid? Surely, there had been signs? He couldn't think of any. How could she do that to him?

A feather-light touch on his arm startled him, and his eyes popped open to find the pink-haired waitress looking up at him.

"Hi," he said.

She smiled, and it was a cute, innocent smile that didn't really match her crazy hair and multiple tattoos. "I've got to get back to work, and you should go, but I thought I should tell you ..." Her eyes bore into his with an unnerving intensity. "I don't think this is over." She pressed her body up against his, and every cell in his body sprang to life as she slid two fingers into the pocket of his jeans. "He's probably still watching right now. Don't try to contact your girlfriend. Call me later. I'll try to help."

She stood on her tiptoes to kiss him on the cheek, but her lips barely made contact with his skin. He found this disappointing. She flashed him another quick smile and then turned to go.

"Wait!" he said and then lowered his voice. "I don't have your number."

She furrowed her brow and whispered, "What do you think I just slipped into your pocket?" Then she smiled again and vanished into the bar.

Oh. That. Well, how was he supposed to know? Talk about sensory overload. He was brokenhearted, disappointed, embarrassed, and confused. He was going to get at least five songs out of the last hour of his life. And then there was Lettie. He obviously wasn't interested in *her.* She was *so* not his type. He started to reach for his pocket and then stopped himself. There was a reason she'd been discreet. He looked around, a little creeped out that he might be being watched, but he didn't see the PI anywhere. He let his hand fall to his side, trying to act naturally, and then he climbed into his pickup. He put the keys in the ignition and then froze, staring at the front of the bar. He didn't want to drive away from Lettie. That was strange. She had her *nose pierced,* for crying out loud. And her hair was pink. Not *at all* the woman he was looking for. He forced himself to start the truck and backed out onto the busy street. Then he drove home, all the while checking in his rearview mirror for someone following him. But he didn't see anyone.

He pulled into the driveway, relieved that his roommates didn't appear to be home. It wasn't that he didn't like them. He did. But he'd spent the last several weeks going on and on about how awesome Natalie was, and how he was going to marry her and move out, and how they should start looking for a new housemate. He didn't want to face them right now. He certainly wasn't going to tell them that he'd found out she was married, but he had to tell them he wasn't going to marry her. They didn't need to find a new housemate.

He could afford to live on his own now, but he'd been living with Rose and Jerry for a few years, since he'd first moved to Nashville, and he spent so much time touring that he didn't want to waste money on his own place. He was comfortable where he was, at least, until he found Mrs. Right. Then he'd need to move out. Then he'd need to spend some of his new money and buy a nice house with a big yard for all the kids they were going to have. He couldn't wait. He checked his phone to see if Natalie had answered him yet. The fact that she hadn't was telling. He'd spent enough time with her to know that she checked her phone with annoying regularity. Wait, maybe *that* had been a clue. He shook his head. Nah, *everyone* checked their phone that often.

He collapsed on his couch, grateful for the comfort of the worn leather. He pulled the slip of paper out of his pocket and unfolded it. He was amused to see that the number was written in pink ink. Then he wondered why this amused him so. He needed to stop acting like he had a crush on the waitress. If anything, these were just rebound emotions. He texted her, "Thanks for your help, I guess. I still don't understand what happened. Let me know when you can talk." Send.

He stared at the phone, waiting for either woman to respond, and then realized he was being pathetic. He stood up to grab his guitar—might as well get started on the Natalie songs. But then his phone beeped. Ashamed of how excited this made him, he looked down.

"Who is this?"

What? This waitress really *was* nuts. Or she had a terrible memory.

"Cole."

No waiting period this time. "Cole who?"

Seriously? "Cole Washburne."

"I don't know any Cole Washburne."

Oh my word. "We met like five minutes ago. I'm the one you forced into the bathroom and then kicked out of the bar."

Nothing. He sat back down and waited. Nothing.

Then he panicked. What if he'd texted the wrong number? That was *not* a cool thing to text to some stranger, especially if that stranger recognized his name. Why had he texted his last name? He felt like hitting himself. Instead, he took a deep breath and double-checked the number. He had gotten it right, so he texted, "Sorry, isn't this the waitress at Maxwell's?"

Like lightening, the response came back, making him wonder how anyone typed that fast. "Waitress is sexist. They're called servers."

He tipped his head back and rested it on the back of the couch. He wished he could undo this whole day. Just go back to bed, wake up, and start over. First thing he would do was *not* meet a married lady for drinks.

His phone dinged again. "Yeah, it's me. I'm just messing with you. I'll call you on my break."

He sighed and tossed his phone aside. She wasn't funny. She probably thought she was funny, but she wasn't. And then he knew he had a lyric. He grabbed his notebook and guitar and started to write. "She thinks she's funny, but she isn't ... she doesn't understand my condition ..." No, that has too many syllables. He erased the second line and then chewed on the pencil. "She thinks she's funny, but she's isn't ... she thought I'd laugh, but I didn't ... everything's a joke when you're carefree, but carefree's not me." Awesome! Now he just needed a melody. He began to strum.

Ninety minutes later, he had a catchy chorus and one and a half verses, and his phone rang with the chorus of "Cleanin' This Gun." Not because he ever planned on shooting his manager, but because his manager looked a lot like Rodney Atkins.

"Hi, Shawn."

"Hey, Cole. Listen, I just got a call from *Country Scoop.*"

Cole's stomach dove for the floor.

"I'm confident there's no truth to this, but they asked if you were dating a woman by the name of Natalie Miller?"

Miller? She'd told him her name was Natalie *Green*. Maybe *that's* why she said she wasn't on Facebook. Suddenly, there *were* signs. He'd just been too stupid to see them. He cleared his throat. He didn't know what to say. He couldn't lie to his manager.

"I'm sorry, Shawn. She led me to believe she wasn't married." How could he be such a moron? "I just found out, and I won't see her again."

Shawn made a grunting noise Cole hadn't heard before. "That's a serious problem, Cole."

"I know. I'm sorry."

"I'm sure you are. But I'm also sure this could turn into a brand nightmare. You're the good, old-fashioned, cowboy heartthrob. You can't be stealing people's wives—"

"I didn't steal anything!" It was suddenly very hot in his living room.

"I know you didn't mean to, but you've got to be careful—"

"Yeah, I know that now."

"All right. Let's do damage control. Does anyone know?"

He hesitated. "Well, I told my roommates about her, but they don't know she's married, and I'd rather they didn't find out. And then the waitress today, she saw us, and the private investigator I'm assuming Natalie's husband hired. I'm sure he's the one who tipped off the tabloid. But other than that, no one."

"Other than that," Shawn repeated, his voice laden with sarcasm.

"The waitress won't tell anyone, I don't think. She's the one who saved me from being caught. The PI doesn't know for sure that anything was going on."

"Really?"

"Really. He didn't even see me with her. He was just suspicious because, well, I don't know why. He just didn't like me, I guess."

"I guess. Well, that's good news. All right, your official comment is, 'Marriage is sacred. I would never have an affair.' Got it?"

"Got it."

"Good. And you'd better find a date for tonight."

"Yes, sir."

"See you in a few hours."

Cole hung up the phone and started to lie down on the couch for a good sulk, but then "Stranger in My House" rang out from his phone. That was his ringtone for unknown callers. He had to change that, pronto. No more cheating songs for ringtones. No more cheating songs for anything.

"Hello?"

"Hi. It's Lettie, your *server*."

"Yeah, yeah, sorry, I'm not much for PC."

"You're not much for being polite?"

"No, no," he stammered, "I'm all for being polite. I make it a priority, in fact—"

"I'm just messing with you again. Anyway, here's the scoop. Darren Jameson is one of Nashville's many private investigators. He called me and told me he'd be swinging by. I made a quick scan of the place and easily saw that you were the target."

"Wait, why would he call you and tell you that?"

"Because he's my brother, and we don't exactly get along, so he didn't want me to think he was there because of me. He was sort of warning me that he was coming, as in, 'Hey, I'm coming to your place of work, but don't freak out, it's not about you.'"

He was her brother? Yikes!

"Anyway, I recognized you, which is weird, because I could care less about country's newest fads ..."

Wowsa! And she was scolding him for not being polite?

"... pity on you. You're welcome."

Wait, he'd missed something there while he was busy being offended. Or maybe several somethings. "How did you know we were the ones?"

"It was obvious. Country stars only come to Maxwell's if they're trying to lay low. And you obviously weren't trying to lay low. You stuck out like a tourist with your ten-gallon hat on—"

"I'm not a tourist." It was official. He didn't like her. Not one bit. She was rude.

"I didn't say you were a tourist. I said you looked like one. Do you want to hear this or not? Because I've got no skin in this game."

He let out a long breath. "Go ahead."

"So, you obviously weren't worried about being recognized, yet you were at Maxwell's, the only bar in Nashville *without* a stage. And she looked nervous. Kept looking at the door, like she was paranoid."

Really? He hadn't noticed that. "Maybe you should be the private investigator. You're awfully observant for a waitr—" he stopped and corrected himself—"for a *server*."

"Servers have to be observant. If we want tips, anyway. But yes, you're right. Suspicion runs in the family."

What an ominous thing to say. He wasn't sure how to respond. He started to tell her that her PI brother had called the tabloids, but then stopped himself. He didn't know Darren had been the one. He shouldn't accuse him falsely.

4

Lettie could hear Cole breathing over the phone. Was he going to say anything? It was his turn to speak. She gave him his chance, and then gave up. "Okay, then—"

"So what do we do now?"

Oh sure, *now* he decided to speak, once she did. "What do you mean?"

"I mean, what do you think your brother's going to do with his suspicions?"

She felt a pang in her chest. The poor bumpkin. He sounded so sad. "I don't know. You're not going to see her anymore, are you?"

Another long pause. Then, "I guess not. She won't even answer my texts."

"You should stop texting her. She played you for a fool."

"Gee, thanks."

"You're welcome." She bit her lip. She had to stop being so sarcastic. "This can't be easy. I don't mean to be insensitive. My brother is probably just going to continue following her around until he gets photo evidence of something or until her husband stops paying him."

Cole groaned.

She wasn't sure what that meant. "You okay?"

"Yeah, just makes me a little sick to hear the words, 'her husband.' I had planned to be her husband."

"Seriously? How long have you been seeing her?"

"So you think he'll leave me alone then?"

Nice dodge, there, buckaroo. "I really don't know for sure. I wouldn't take anything for granted. If he really thinks you were there with her, he might keep poking his nose into your business, and I doubt he fell for our little ruse, no matter how good your kiss was ... I mean ..." *Oh my soul, what did I just say?* "I mean, you know, how *convincing* the kiss was."

"A-huh." He sounded amused. Awesome. "Well, we might have a little problem."

"Oh yeah? What's that?" She didn't like his use of the word "we."

"I have to go to a very public fundraiser tonight. I'm performing, and then there's an after-party. Going to be lots of press there. If I go alone, and your brother finds out, won't he be suspicious that you didn't go with me?"

It was her turn to groan. "Maybe," she admitted. Then she rushed to add, "Just tell him that I was going to go, and then I was sick."

"So you're willing to stay home tonight and pretend to be sick?"

Just how far did he expect her to take this charade? No, she didn't want to stay home on the couch tonight. She rarely got weekend nights off, and she had plans. "Actually, I had planned to go out with some friends."

He gasped, as if she'd said she planned to beat up her grandmother. "You can't!"

"I most certainly can! I'm not the one who got you into this mess!" There was that pang in her chest again. Why did she have so much compassion for this guy? Was it because he smelled like cedar shavings? A vivid vision flashed in her brain: the wedding. *Oh shoot.* She'd forgotten all about it. She had to go to her cousin's wedding the next day. Would Darren be there? She had no idea. He wasn't much for social gatherings, especially ones that involved family. If he *was* there, though, would he expect to see Cole there? What a mess she'd gotten herself into.

Then, like a dark cloud crossing over the wedding image in her mind, Jason entered the scene. Her stomach sank. He wouldn't be there, probably. But if he *was* there, maybe it would be good to have a big, strapping fake boyfriend on her—

"Please? Come with me. It will be fun. You can meet some big stars, like Dierks—"

"I could give a hoot less about any big country stars. I don't even like music." She paused. "I really don't want to go." She didn't, did she? "You don't really need me to, do you?" He did, didn't he? She should go. Not because she wanted to, not because he smelled good, but because it was the right thing to do. She wondered what the male equivalent of a damsel in distress was. Because he was it.

"I'm not sure what I need right now. I've never been caught in an extramarital affair." He sounded miserable.

A thought occurred to her. "Didn't it make you suspicious that your girlfriend"—she realized her voice was thick with sarcasm and tried to tone it back—"wouldn't go to this fundraiser thing?"

She heard him swallow. "She said she was going to. I was so excited to show her off to everyone. But then, right before you ambushed me—"

"Ambushed?" she cried, indignant. "I rescued you! You're welcome!"

"Right before you ambushed me," he said again, over-enunciating the offending word, "she told me that she had to work, and wouldn't be able to make it after all."

Lettie bit back a laugh. "And where does she work?"

"General Hospital. She's a nurse ... I think."

The poor sucker. "What would I need to wear?" She decided not to mention the wedding. Let's see if she could even stand the guy first.

"You'll go?"

"I didn't say that. I doubt I have anything to wear."

"You can wear anything you want."

She snickered. He had no idea what he'd just given her permission to do. She had a Punk Rave dress that was sure to get him on the front page of the tabloids. But she wouldn't do that to him. Or would she? Maybe she would. "What time?"

"Show starts at eight, but I would need to be there early. I could pick you up at six-thirty?"

She got out at six. That didn't give her much time to find an outfit. "If you honestly don't care what I show up in, sure, pick me up. I'll text you my address."

"I honestly don't care. Just don't wear orange. It will clash with your pink hair."

Was the cowboy trying to be funny? Despite herself, she smiled. "Orange it is then."

5

As soon as Cole hung up the phone, he opened his Facebook app and looked up Natalie Miller. And there she was, all smiles, sitting in a pile of leaves with two kids. His stomach cramped. There were children. How could there be children? How could he not have known? And there was a picture of her with a man who was probably the husband. The private investigator-hiring husband. He couldn't decide which was worse: his heartbreak or his guilt. He stabbed at the screen to close the app. He couldn't take much more of that.

He tried to finish the Lettie's-not-funny song, but he was no longer in the mood. Now when he thought about her, he felt mostly gratitude. Gratitude and a small fear about what she was going to wear.

"WOWSA! YOU LOOK AMAZING!" He couldn't believe his eyes. She wore a short lipstick-red sleeveless dress that showed off her tattoos and definitely clashed with her pink hair, which was curled up into a neat bun that showed how thick her hair was. He wondered what it might be like to run his fingers through it, and then wondered why on earth he'd just wondered that.

"You don't have to sound so surprised." She gave him a wry smile and stepped outside, quietly closing the door behind her. Her lavender lipstick seemed to glow in the early evening light. He would have found purple lips disturbing on anyone else, but on her they somehow seemed perfect. She looked him up and down. "And you look ... exactly the same."

"I'm sorry. I just didn't know what to expect. You made it sound like you had nothing to wear."

"I didn't. I only own three dresses. I'm glad this one is good enough."

He opened his truck door. "It's plenty good enough. You look great."

She appeared to be surprised that he had opened the door for her and hesitated before climbing in. He offered her a hand, which she shyly took, and pushed herself up into the cab. He clicked the door shut behind her, thinking maybe this evening wouldn't be so bad. Sure, people would be surprised when he showed up with a purple-lipped date, but suddenly, he wasn't afraid to shake things up. At least she wasn't married.

He climbed into the other side of the truck and started the engine.

She immediately reached over and turned his radio off. If it had been anyone else, he would have been horribly offended. In fact, his friends and family back home never would have dared to do such a thing, but this wasn't Wyoming, and Lettie wasn't friends and family.

"We can listen to whatever you want. Doesn't have to be that station."

"No, thank you. I prefer silence."

He didn't know how to answer that. Did she mean silence from music or silence altogether? Did she not want him to speak? If so, she was going to be disappointed. He was too anxious to be quiet. "You say you don't like music, but you choose to live in Music City?"

"I know, ironic, right? You know how people say, 'No one from Nashville is from Nashville'? Well, I am. I grew up here. I'm an actual local. For better or worse, this is my hometown. Every city has its flaws, but thankfully, there is more to Nashville than music."

He tried to focus on driving. There was even more traffic than usual, which was saying something, as traffic was always atrocious at this time of night, and her presence was making him nervous. "Well, unfortunately, there's going to be a lot of music tonight."

"I know." He could hear the smile in her voice without looking at her. "But I won't hold that against you."

He eased to a stop in front of a red light and then looked at her.

She batted her eyelashes, but he sensed that she hadn't done it on purpose. "What?"

He shrugged one shoulder and looked at the light. "I just can't imagine not liking music. I mean, I guess I can imagine not liking country. Actually, I can't. But I can accept that some people prefer other genres. But not liking music altogether? That just baffles me." He glanced at her out of the corner of his eye, and she was staring at him with the most genuine expression on her face. He didn't think there would be any pretense with this woman. She was who she was. This realization made him even more nervous to be around her.

"I blame sixth-grade saxophone lessons."

He laughed. "Yeah, I've heard that's not the easiest instrument to master."

"I didn't get anywhere near mastering it. My mom wanted me to play the guitar, so I rebelled by signing up for the saxophone at school. It was the most expensive instrument on the list in band class." She snickered. "I lasted the year, but I don't think I ever learned more than three notes, and those three notes were pretty squeaky."

The light finally turned green. "That's too bad. I've never jammed out with a sax player before. It'd be fun." He flashed her a quick smile.

"Oh, trust me, I was never a sax player."

"So, your mom played guitar?"

"Yeah, so who is performing tonight?"

The air in the truck seemed to tighten. Had she just avoided his question? "I thought you didn't care."

"I don't. Just trying to make conversation."

He put on his blinker. "Dierks Bentley, Scotty McCreery, Emily Ann Roberts, Maren Morris, and yours truly. There may be a few more, but that's who I remember."

"Never heard of any of those people." She so obviously didn't care.

Maybe she wasn't so genuine. No way she hadn't heard of Dierks Bentley. "Well, they are some pretty big names. And you knew who I was."

"I didn't know your name," she said quickly. "I just recognized your face."

"Oh yeah? Why's that?"

She hesitated. "Not sure. I do live here, though. Must have seen you around."

He pulled into the venue's back lot and rolled down his window to talk to the parking attendant.

"Wow, there sure are a lot of people here."

The attendant waved him through.

"Yeah, I told you. It's a pretty big event. I was lucky to get the invite. Going to be some bigwigs here, and I need all the help I can get."

Her head snapped toward him. "Seriously?"

"Yeah, why?"

She shrugged and looked away. "I don't know. I guess I kind of thought you were fairly bigwigged yourself."

6

A couple of relaxed security guards ushered them through a back door, and Cole seamlessly led them to a large room full of fancy furniture. *He must have been here before*, Lettie thought. The room was full of people, and despite herself, she felt nervous knowing she was rubbing elbows with celebrities. Cole began introducing her as "his friend Lettie," and everyone was cordial, but it was all a bit of a blur. She didn't recognize any of the names Cole fired off.

As soon as she got a chance, she pulled on his arm. He leaned his ear closer to her lips, and she had an insane urge to kiss him on the cheek, an urge she managed to suppress. "You keep calling me your friend," she whispered. "Shouldn't you be saying 'girlfriend'?"

He nodded. "Yeah, I s'pose you're right. Guess I just didn't want to presume."

She held her hands out to her side, palms up, and shrugged. "Presume away." Then she tried to give him a reassuring smile. She wasn't sure why this mattered to her, but she wanted this mission to be successful. Maybe she was just trying to outwit her brother.

A familiar-looking man approached them. "Shawn!" Cole said, obviously excited to see this person. "This is my date, Lettie. Lettie, this is my manager, Shawn."

Well, still not "girlfriend," but "date" is better than "friend." She stuck out her hand. "Nice to meet you."

"Pleasure's all mine." He pumped her hand up and down with an enthusiasm she found excessive.

She tried to pull her hand away, but he held on. Because she didn't know what else to say, she said, "You look familiar. Have we met?"

He finally dropped her hand.

"Nah," Cole said, "he just looks like Rodney Atkins."

She had no idea who that was. "Who?"

Shawn laughed, his eyes flitting between their faces. "Seriously? Rodney Atkins?"

She shrugged.

Cole put his arm around her shoulders, almost protectively. "She's not much of a country fan."

"I see, I see," Shawn said, still smiling. "Well, let's get you to sound check, Cole."

"Yes, sir." He pulled her closer to him. "You okay to hang out here? Make yourself comfortable? Get a drink—"

"I don't drink," she snapped, and instantly felt guilty. "I mean, no thank you."

He chuckled uncomfortably. "I don't drink either. So, see? We do have something in common."

"Could I come with you to sound check?" The quiver in her voice embarrassed her. There were just far too many rhinestones in the room for her comfort.

"Sure, I guess. It's not going to be very exciting." He gave her a chance to change her mind, but she didn't, so he said, "Come on." He led her out of the room and down a cement hallway, his hand still lightly resting across her shoulders. As they got closer to the stage, she could hear drums and bass. They rounded a corner and met a herd of people holding cameras and microphones.

"Cole!" the closest woman cried. "Are the allegations true?" She shoved a recorder into his face. "Is this your mistress?"

Her hand flew to her face to shield her eyes from the flashing cameras, but she was also instinctively trying to hide her face. It was no use, though, as the people surrounded her. They were talking at Cole, but they were looking at her, taking her picture, pressing in so close they were touching her. She broke out in a sweat that she knew was going to wreak havoc on her makeup, and she breathed faster and faster until she felt as though she wasn't getting any air at all. She pressed into Cole, and his arm slid around her waist. She didn't think anything had ever felt as good as that arm: real, strong, sturdy, safe. For a second, she didn't care that he was a hillbilly musician; for a second, she would have married him if it meant keeping his arm in that spot. She realized he was pulling her through the mob, and she willed her legs to move. Vaguely, she could hear him talking, but it sounded as though he was much farther away than he was: "No, this is my girlfriend, Lettie. No, I would never get involved with a married woman. No, the rumors are just rumors. Marriage is sacred." He had to physically push people out of the way to get the door open, but then the two of them were through it, and she heard the blessed *whoosh* of it closing behind them. She leaned back on it and promptly burst into tears.

"There, there, Lettie. I'm so, so sorry. It's okay, it's okay."

"Why didn't you tell me?" she snapped.

"I'm sorry," he said again.

She forced herself to look at him. "Everyone knows about your little secret? Why didn't you tell me?"

"It's not my little secret," he said through clenched teeth. "It's not true, remember?" He put his hands on his hips, opened his mouth, and looked at the floor. "I'm sorry. I didn't know this many people had gotten a hold of it. I only knew that one reporter had, and I hoped it would die without evidence."

She snorted. "Obviously not."

"And I didn't want to tell you because if I did, I thought you'd think I was accusing your brother."

Oh. That hadn't even occurred to her. "Are you?"

He didn't answer her, and she knew that he thought Darren was the leak. But this theory didn't offend her. Darren probably was the leak. He hated country music and country artists almost as much as she did.

"Can you please forgive me?" And then that same amazing arm was sliding around her waist again and pulling her away from the door and into him.

She realized there were people in this room too, and they were looking at her, but they looked concerned, not predatory, and then she was pressing her cheek into his shoulder and trying to catch her breath. *Oh my soul, I'm hugging a cedar tree.* Still, she didn't let go. She just concentrated on her breathing and enjoyed the feeling of him rubbing her back. He was really nice. Why did he have to be a stupid musician? She could even put up with the stupid hat, but she could never, *ever* put up with the guitar. No matter how nice he was or how good he smelled. She pushed herself off him and looked up at him. "Didn't mean to freak out on you." She wiped at her eyes, trying not to further destroy her eye makeup.

"It's totally understandable," he said softly. She thought he was trying to keep the gawkers from hearing him. He rubbed her shoulder, and she jerked it away. His face fell, and she felt guilty.

She took a deep breath. "I don't know how you stand it."

He looked at the closed doors behind them. "That's the worst it's ever been for me." He rubbed his jaw, and she noticed then how big it was, how strong it looked. "Hope it's true that there's no such thing as bad publicity."

Over his shoulder, she saw Shawn approaching them. "I think they're ready for you."

Cole turned around and held up one finger. "Just a sec." He took her hand and led her toward the chairs. She wondered if he was trying to play the part or if he really wanted to hold her hand. She had to stop this. After tonight, they had to stage a breakup. Ah, shoot, the wedding. Okay, maybe after the wedding. He led her to a section marked reserved, and gestured toward the seats. "Take your pick. I've got to go up on stage for sound check, but then I'll come back and join you, or we can go back to the reception room if you want."

No way. She was *not* going back through that herd. "Only if there's a sneaky back way."

He smiled and shook his head. "That's what I figured. We'll just stay here. That's okay. The show will start in less than an hour." He turned to go then, and she panicked a little at being left alone. What was wrong with her? She prided herself on her emotional stability, her inner strength. Why was this experience turning her into a mental mushroom? She sat down, folded her arms across her chest, and stared at the stage.

7

The doors opened, and the people flooded in. The reserved seating area they were in kept some of the attendees at bay, but plenty still came to take selfies with Cole and ask for his autograph. He introduced most of them to Lettie, and made a big deal of her being his girlfriend. Some of them looked surprised, and he didn't know if this was because they were expecting him to be hiding his mistress or because his new girlfriend looked like a punk rocker. He could tell Lettie was uncomfortable with all the attention, and he felt bad about that, but there wasn't much he could do. He had to be nice to these people. They weren't necessarily his fans, yet, but he certainly wanted them to be. If he could get all of Dierks's people to love him, he'd be a superstar.

Eventually, the other artists trickled in, and the attention the patrons gave him thinned out as they started paying attention to the other celebrities. He sat down beside Lettie and thanked her for her patience.

"I didn't realize singers got to sit in the audience," she said without looking at him.

He had the urge to put his hand on her knee, an urge which surprised him. "We don't, usually, but where this is a benefit, most of us will be out here for most of the show. I'm only singing three songs tonight. So the rest of the time, I'll be sitting right here enjoying the show."

She looked at him. "And do you?"

"Do I what?"

"Enjoy it. I mean, it's your whole life. Surely you don't still enjoy sitting watching other people sing?"

What was she getting at? "If it's good music, of course I enjoy it. There's nothing better."

She grimaced and returned her eyes to the empty stage.

"Hey, you okay?"

She shrugged. "I guess. I just don't get it."

He felt guilty. He'd dragged her into such a mess. "You know, you can go if you want. I can tell people you weren't feeling well. You've already made a very public appearance, and I'm grateful. You don't have to stay for the whole show."

She stared at him as if she was thinking it over. Finally, she said, "Nah. Thank you, but I don't want to be that much of a jerk. Besides, I might need a favor from you one day." She smiled, but it looked forced. "I want you to really owe me." She reached out and patted his knee, but then snatched her hand away. Too bad.

The house lights dimmed, and people scrambled to find their seats. He missed Lettie's hand. He would definitely do her a favor. In fact, he looked forward to it.

An emcee came out on stage to polite applause, welcomed everyone, thanked them for buying tickets to support a good cause, and then introduced the first singer, Kelsey Snapp. Cole had heard the name before, but he didn't think he'd seen her perform.

She strode out onto the stage, and Cole was delighted to see she had a pink streak in her hair. Maybe pink hair wasn't so strange after all. He'd never really given it much thought. Of course, she had just *one* streak, with *one* shade of pink. Not quite Lettie's level of chaos.

Kelsey began to sing, and he tried to tune in, but his mind kept drifting toward the woman beside him. He caught himself looking at her legs and forced his eyes back to the stage. Why was he feeling all warm and fuzzy about this woman? Sure, he was grateful to her for all her help—she might have even saved his career before it ever got going—but he had to get a grip. She was *so* not his type. And he feared she was a little crazy.

She looked at him suddenly and caught him gawking at her, and he jerked his face front so fast that it screamed guilt. *Golly, I am such a dork. What is this, junior high?*

Kelsey finished up, and he leaned over to whisper to Lettie. When he did, a few stray curls that had escaped her bun tickled his cheek. It felt wonderful. "I've got to go. I'll be right back."

She nodded and gave him a small smile that looked shyer than usual. He returned the favor and then got up to awkwardly shuffle out of the row. Then he made his way backstage as he heard the next performer start to sing.

Shawn met him in the wings.

"Why are you back here?" Cole asked. "I thought you'd be out front watching the show."

Shawn wiggled his phone at him. "I thought you'd like an update. You and your date are all over the place. Looks like people are buying it—"

"Buying what? She really is my date."

Shawn looked skeptical, and Cole realized he'd been too defensive. "Anyway, there's still some chatter about your alleged affair, but without corroborating sources, I think this is going to die a natural death. Good job, kiddo." Shawn slapped him on the arm, but Cole was completely absorbed in thinking about Natalie.

He wanted to see her one last time, to make sure it was really true. He had so many questions. Why had she picked him to be the sucker? And did she ever really care about him? He slid his guitar strap over his shoulder and headed for the spotlight. *Never mind all that,* he told himself. *Better to pretend it never even happened.*

He gave the audience his broadest smile. "Good evening, folks. I'm Cole Washburne."

They answered him with a soft golf clap, but he'd take it. The band started up, and he started to pick. Then he leaned into the microphone to sing his only single. "I've known certain things all my life ... like it'll rain on game day ... and every man needs a good wife ... I've had dreams ... I've had visions ... made the white picket fence my mission." He took a big breath and then threw himself into the chorus: "Oh yeah, I can see the future ... I'm no psychic, I'm no prophet, just a cowboy with a promise ... the American dream ... tailor-made for me ... oh yeah, I can see the future."

Some people cheered during the chorus. This was encouraging, though he figured some of them were probably just realizing they'd heard the song before. He looked at Lettie, but her face was impassive. Oh well, too late to turn back now. It was time for verse two. "All I've ever wanted to have ... good land, good food ... and a life like my own dad had ... I've had dreams ... I've had visions ... a good wife, two kids, and plenty of fishin' ..."

The crowd cheered louder during the second chorus. They were warming up to him. That was a good thing, because Lettie didn't appear to be. He belted out the bridge for all he was worth.

8

Lettie stared up at her fake date and couldn't believe how confident he seemed. *He must really feel at home up there.*

"I can see the beautiful woman, and she thinks I'm just grand," he belted into the microphone, "I can see the kids playing in a box full of sand. I can see the dog chasing the stick. I can see the house, the truck, the whole kit ... and caboodle. Oh yeah ... I can see the future."

Kit and caboodle? These lyrics were ridiculous. He was like something straight out of the fifties, only his jeans were tighter. This made her think of James Dean. There was a resemblance there, except that she'd never seen Cole with a cigarette, and his hair wasn't quite as poofy. She returned her focus to the song's words. Was this just a song, or did he actually feel this way? Was he just trying to make his audience happy, or did he really want to live in an episode of *Leave It to Beaver*? She hoped it was the former, but realizing that she hoped this surprised her. What did she care if he wanted to marry a Stepford Wife? That was nothing to her. Yet the idea made her a little sick to her stomach.

He finished the picket fence anthem and paused for applause. Then the stage lights dimmed, and he began a soft ballad about lost love. He did have a good voice, though she thought probably his good looks contributed more to his rise to stardom than his talent did. He certainly looked the part, with his broad shoulders, thick thighs, and round butt—*ack!* What was she doing? She didn't need to be thinking about his butt. As he expounded on what it feels like to have one's heart ripped out of one's chest, she thought she heard him get a little choked up. Her heart swelled with compassion for him. His heart had been broken, and he couldn't even talk to anyone about it, because he had to pretend it had never happened. Or maybe he was just acting.

Maybe it was just a sad song, and he was just good at performing it. Her compassion vanished, and she felt better.

His third song was a painful, upbeat rockabilly ditty about boots: from cowboy boots and dancing boots to muck boots and duck boots. She had no idea what a duck boot was. Why would a duck wear boots? Still, it was catchy, and the crowd seemed to be into it, chair dancing and tapping their toes. The tune certainly did give Cole ample chance to twitch his—and there she was, back to his butt. She had to stop.

He finished singing, and the crowd erupted in applause. She thought they were clapping more for him than they had the previous acts, but maybe she was just biased. With what looked like a well-practiced wave, Cole left the stage and was replaced by a woman she didn't recognize. The crowd certainly knew her, though. At least everyone else was happy. Lettie wished she had some chocolate.

During the new woman's second song, Cole slid into the seat beside her, and she was taken aback by how happy she was to see him. He wasn't chocolate, but he was a close second.

"Good job up there," she whispered. "You're a natural."

He smiled. "Thank you." He stared into her eyes, and his gaze made her nervous.

She returned her eyes to the stage and tried to focus on the show. It wasn't long before she wished she hadn't. The woman was singing a song that compared country music to religion, and Lettie's stomach cramped. She tried to stop listening to the lyrics, but it was too late. A fat tear slid down her cheek before she realized it had even formed, and she slapped it away with the back of her hand.

Cole put his hand on her leg and leaned toward her. "Are you okay?"

She nodded quickly, without looking at him.

"I know it's a pretty moving song."

She looked at him then. "No, it's not," she snapped. His head recoiled in surprise, and she felt bad. She tried to think of something to say that would undo the damage and came up with, "It's a stupid song."

This did not undo anything. "I love this song, and so do all these people." He looked around the room.

She followed his gaze. He was right. The crowd appeared to be enraptured. This just made her stomach pain worse. She closed her eyes and tried to think about something else, tried to will the evening to be over.

9

Cole had enjoyed the evening. He wished he could say the same for his fake date. She was obviously miserable. In the dark of his cab, fighting the traffic, he tried to think of something intelligent to say. "I'm sorry you didn't have fun. When you said you didn't like music, I didn't realize you would hate tonight as much as you did."

"I didn't hate it," she said quickly. "Okay, maybe I did. But that's not your fault, and you don't need to be sorry. I just have my issues. You did really well. I was proud to be with you."

Her words made his chest warm. "Thank you. That's quite a compliment coming from you. Not to get too personal, but why did you get so upset during the—"

"That song irritated the snot out of me."

Despite himself, he chuckled. "Tell me how you really feel."

"I have a tendency to tell it like it is, or at least, how it is to *me*. I don't mean to offend you, or that singer, or anyone. But country music is not religion. It is not God. It is just an industry. When people fall down and worship it, people get hurt." Her voice cracked on the last word.

"Have you been hurt by country music?" he asked gently.

She snorted as if that were preposterous. "Of course not. I have never wanted anything to do with country music."

"Okay, it's none of my business. But you didn't just sound like someone who hasn't ever had anything to do with country. You sound like you know a little bit about the industry."

She didn't say anything, and he didn't want to pry. They rode along in silence, starting and stopping at the lights. Finally, he pulled into the driveway of her apartment building. Suddenly, he felt very nervous. "May I walk you to your door?"

She giggled, sounding pretty nervous herself. "You don't have to do that."

What did that mean? He knew he didn't have to do that. But did she want him to? He sat there like a confused chump and then realized she had climbed out of the truck by herself. Shoot, he'd meant to get the door for her. He jumped out and hurried around, getting there just in time to help her shut the door. Well, since he was out of the truck now, he might as well walk her to her door. He hurried ahead to open the outside door for her and then walked awkwardly beside her to the door of apartment two.

She turned to face him, and he panicked. She didn't expect him to kiss her, did she? Of course not. This wasn't a real date. "Cole?" she said softly, the sweetness in her voice making his heart race. "Would you do me a huge favor?"

Oh wow, she did want him to kiss her. He wished he'd eaten a breath mint. "Sure." He tried to sound confident when he felt anything but.

She took a deep breath. "Okay, feel free to say no. I know you don't really owe me anything. I mean, I did you a favor, but this really hasn't been a big deal. So don't feel like you have to do this, but I thought I would just ask, I mean, just in case you're willing—"

He interrupted her with a laugh. "Wow, do you need my firstborn? Just go ahead and ask, Lettie."

Her cheeks flushed pink, and she looked at the floor.

He reached out and touched her elbow. "Hey," he said softly. "I didn't mean to embarrass you. I just felt bad that you were so nervous to ask me. Go ahead. I really do owe you, and even if I didn't, I'd like to help you out."

She exhaled slowly. "I have to go to my cousin's wedding tomorrow. I don't think my brother will be there, but he might be. I mean, he might go just to see if you go. But even if he's not part of the equation, I could still use your company." Something in her tone suggested there was more to the story.

He wanted to push for details, but it didn't matter what those details were. He would go no matter what they were, and he could get those details on the way to the wedding. "Okay, sure, what time?"

Her eyes widened. "Really? You'll go?"

"Sure. What time?"

"The wedding's at three. But it's an hour away. I can drive, though."

"That's okay, I've seen your car." He chuckled, but then felt guilty. He hadn't meant to insult her car. Besides, it might be in way better shape than it had looked. "Unless of course you want to drive, in which case, sure, you can drive."

She shook her head slightly. "No, you're right. We'd probably be safer in your truck." She raised an eyebrow. "Of course, I could drive that."

He laughed. "We can discuss that tomorrow. How about if I get here at quarter of two. Would that work for you?"

"That would be awesome. Thanks, Cole." She turned and hurried into her apartment, closing the door behind her as she said good night, leaving him standing there in the hallway with no time to struggle over whether to kiss her. Part of him was relieved. Part of him was disappointed. Part of him was excited to see her again tomorrow. He loved weddings.

10

I hate weddings, Lettie thought as Cole pulled his truck into the church parking lot. She hadn't been to many, but all the marriages she'd witnessed the birth of had since died in divorce. No matter how persuasive Cole's lyrics were, she didn't have much faith in the institution of marriage. Quite the opposite, in fact.

Cole jumped out of the truck and raced around to beat her to the door handle. She rolled her eyes at his antiquated chivalry, but the action warmed her heart. At least he was trying to be sweet, even if his methods were a teeny bit sexist. He offered her a hand, and she took it. Then she slid out of the truck, suddenly aware that people in the parking lot were staring at her. At first, this alarmed her, but then she thought maybe they recognized Cole. How bizarre. He wasn't *that* big of a star, was he?

He let go of her hand, shut the truck door, and then put his hand to the small of her back, which sent shivers up her spine. And together, they headed toward the large white building. She couldn't even really identify *why*, but she was so glad Cole was there with her. Even if Jason didn't show up, she was still glad.

But then there he was. They'd just stepped into the foyer, and her eyes were still adjusting to the indoor lighting, when she made eye contact with him. He was more than a hundred feet away, and yet he still made her blood run cold. She grabbed hold of Cole's arm, not for the show, but to steady herself.

An usher offered them a program, and she ripped her eyes away from Jason's gaze. "Would you like to sit on the bride's side or the groom's?" the usher asked.

There was an elongated pause as she realized Cole wasn't going to answer the question. He didn't even know the answer to the question. "Uh ... the groom's," she said quickly.

"Great. Right this way."

They followed the elderly gentleman down the red-carpeted aisle and grew closer and closer to Jason. She wanted to say something, make Cole laugh, make it look like they were madly in love. "You've always dreamed about being on the red carpet, right?" she said, and thank the heavens, he did laugh. She pulled his arm closer to her and laughed right along with him, but her laugh came out sounding a little like a lunatic's, and he looked down at her with a concerned frown. "Uh," she said to the usher, who was still leading them closer to the front, "can we sit back here? We're not super close to the groom. Don't want to take up the family's seats."

He nodded, though he looked a little confused. "Of course. You can sit wherever you want, but I don't think Michael has much family coming."

Grateful, she slid into the tenth pew, and Cole followed her in.

"You're not close to the groom? I thought he was your cousin?"

"Okay, don't look, but to your left, about five more rows up, there's a man standing up."

Cole looked.

She elbowed him. "I said don't look!"

"Sorry." He didn't sound the least bit sorry. "What about him?"

"Well, he's sort of my psychotic ex-boyfriend. I don't even know the groom. Never even seen him before. Not even friends on Facebook. But I didn't want to sit anywhere near Jason, so I said we were here for the groom."

"Psychotic?" Cole repeated, his voice heavy with concern. "What does that mean? Was he abusive?"

"He never hit me," she muttered. She almost wished he had. That would have made things simpler. "At first, he was fine. I really liked him, but then he started to get really possessive and controlling, and so I broke up with him. And then he went nuts. Started stalking me. Doing all kinds of creepy things. I don't think he's dangerous." She wasn't so sure.

"What's he doing here?"

"He married my best friend."

"*Married* her? So then, he shouldn't be bothering you anymore, right?"

She shook her head slightly. She could still feel Jason's eyes on her. "Nope. He only married her because of me. I don't know if he did it to make me jealous or to try to have a reason to get close to me." She swallowed hard. She knew how this must sound. "And he kept right on stalking me. She has no idea. He's convinced her I'm the crazy person." She paused, but then thought it necessary to add, "But I'm not."

He chuckled. "I know you're not." He looked at Jason again. She wished he'd stop doing that. As if he read her mind, he turned to face her. "Do you want me to do anything?"

She smiled at him. "No. Thank you, though. I think you just being here might deter him from approaching me. I guarantee that he is *only* here because I am. His wife, Britney, knows the bride, but they're not that close." Cole didn't say anything, and Lettie sensed he didn't believe her. "See? That's how he works. He operates so close to reality that people think his version of life is real. It *almost* makes sense that they're here. But not really, not if you know the real reality of the situation." She looked at Cole. It was so obvious he didn't believe her. She felt like crying. "Fine. Don't believe me."

He put a hand on her leg, and her arms broke out in goosebumps. "I believe you," he said gently.

But she knew he didn't.

The mother of the bride approached. She was wearing a lavender gown with so many frills Lettie thought it would probably out-frill the wedding gown.

"Hi, Aunt Alice."

"Hi, Loretta," she said without an ounce of joy.

Lettie stood for the obligatory hug.

Alice gave her the shortest hug in the history of hugs. They barely touched. This was fine with Lettie, and she sat back down.

"Why did you wear all black to my daughter's wedding?" Alice looked her up and down.

"Everything I own is black."

Alice's face was a knot of disapproval. She looked at Cole. "And who is your friend?"

"This is my boyfriend, Cole," she said loudly.

Cole stood and offered his hand. "Cole Washburne, ma'am. It's a pleasure to meet you. You look lovely. And congratulations."

Her expression softened as she slowly took his hand. "My, my. You are a polite one. What are you doing with my impertinent niece?"

Cole sat back down and put his arm around her. "Aw, she's not so bad." He flashed a smile at her that made her insides all squishy. "I find her charming."

Alice made a tsk tsk sound with her tongue. "If you say so. To each his own, I suppose." She turned her gaze back to Lettie. "And why are you sitting on Michael's side?"

"There seemed to be more people here for Valerie than for Michael. I felt bad. Wanted to balance things out."

Alice's expression suggested she didn't believe this for a second. But she must not have cared to learn the real reason, as she sauntered off toward her side of the sanctuary.

Cole nudged her with his elbow. She looked at him, and he had one gorgeous eyebrow raised. "Loretta?"

She smiled. "Yeah. I'm named after Loretta Lynn, but I've been called Lettie since forever, so don't get any ideas."

He stared at her, a smirk frozen on his face. "You are named after Loretta Lynn, but you hate country music?"

"I don't just hate *country* music. I hate all music. I don't discriminate."

"You hate Christmas carols?"

"Definitely."

"You hate the happy birthday song?"

She snickered. "Yep. And I don't want to—"

"You're on the wrong side," a familiar voice said.

She looked up as she tried to push her body further into the pew, further away from the man standing in front of her. There was a long, awful pause as the two stared each other down.

Cole stuck his hand out. "Cole Washburne."

Jason didn't accept his handshake, and after a few seconds, Cole dropped his arm. "I know who you are," Jason said in a sinister tone, all the while smiling for show. He looked down at Lettie. "Thought you hated singers?"

She didn't give him the satisfaction of a response.

Cole stood up slowly, and Lettie was happy to see he had a few inches on Jason. He leaned toward Jason and said with a level voice, "Go back to your seat, right now."

Jason backed up a few inches and then tried to look tough. "Or what?"

"Do you really want to find out?"

Jason stared at him for a few seconds, then glared at Lettie, and then returned to his side of the sanctuary, and Lettie thought maybe she was in love with Cole Washburne.

11

The reception was held in the church's fellowship hall, and Cole could hear the air conditioners roaring, but it was still hot as hot can be, leaving Cole to wonder why any self-respecting Tennessean would get married in the summer. He could tell Lettie was miserable and wondered why she'd bothered to come. When they had gone through the receiving line, it was obvious that the bride could have cared less whether Lettie was there or not. Now here they were at the reception, probably the only two sober adults in the room. Cole had tried to consume enough deviled eggs to make the whole ordeal worth his while, but they'd stopped refilling the platter. It was just as well, as the cake looked awesome, and he needed to save some room. Now he just sat there holding a limp paper cup of flat punch, fervently hoping no one had noticed how many paprika-laden eggs he'd taken. Didn't need *that* getting into the tabloids.

"Are you sure I can't get you anything?"

Lettie had shown no interest in any of the food. She shook her head, but her blank stare suggested she hadn't even heard the question.

He gently touched her forearm, and her head whipped around. "Hey, sorry, didn't mean to startle you. But, do you just want to go? You're obviously not having any fun."

She turned away from him and stared off into the distance again. "If we leave now, he'll think he scared me away."

Cole could not decide what to make of this whole ex-boyfriend mess. She hadn't given him many details, but those she'd provided made absolutely no sense. No one marries a woman just to get close to another woman. "What's your best friend's name again?"

"She's not my best friend. Not anymore. And her name is Britney."

He waited for her to say more.

She didn't.

"And why aren't you friends anymore?"

She gave an almost imperceptible shrug and shifted uncomfortably in her metal folding chair. "When I heard Jason and her were seeing each other, I tried to warn her. She thought, or he convinced her, probably, that I was just jealous. She hasn't spoken to me since. I wasn't even invited to the wedding."

"So his plan backfired then?" The marriage certainly hadn't gotten him any closer to Lettie.

She gave him a patronizing look he didn't appreciate. "I don't know what his plan was, I never do, so I never know if one is working."

He tried to think of something to say that would cheer her up. He couldn't stand seeing her like this. She was acting like a shell of herself. "Maybe he really is in love with her? Maybe he's moved on?"

Her head snapped toward him again. "Can we talk about something else?"

Okay, fine. He'd shut up then. He was just trying to be nice.

There was some commotion, the music stopped playing, and then someone with a microphone began to announce the wedding party, who were entering on the far end of the room. One by one, the groomsmen and bridesmaids were announced, and then the newly crowned Mr. and Mrs. Michael Tate entered. The bride wore a huge smile. She seemed to be enjoying all the cameras. Her eyes scanned the room and then startled him by landing right on him. She let out a little squeal and let go of her new husband's arm to run at him. *Uh-oh.* Her heels clicked on the floor as most of the crowd turned to see what she was running toward.

Like a reluctant psychic, Cole saw the great catastrophe happening before it did, but there was nothing he could do. An extension cord had been taped to the floor, but dozens of kids running around the room had loosened the safety measure. At least two of the children had tripped over it with their little toes and gone sprawling. They'd bounced up and kept running, and no one had paid them any mind. But they were kids. He feared the bride might not be so bouncy. Her toe caught, and gravity took control of the situation. It impressed Cole how firmly the smile stayed in place. She was more than halfway to the ground before the smile widened into a horrified gape. The bouquet flew out of her hands, headed straight for an elderly woman with a walker, who, bizarrely, let go of the walker with both hands and caught the bouquet. He would have laughed, but there wasn't time. He cringed as the unlucky bride went the rest of the way to the floor, crying out in embarrassment, pain, or both. She put her hands out to break her fall, and some part of her enormous dress made a deafening ripping sound.

The room was silent. The bride whimpered. The groom rushed to her aid and helped her up. As he did, Cole shielded his eyes from the potential reveal a ripped wedding dress might provide, but the dress seemed intact. Whatever had ripped, it hadn't been fatal. She stood up, checked her hair, which hadn't even budged, and then waved to the crowd. "I'm okay, I'm okay!" Her voice quivered. Then she turned to Cole, and his heart stopped. She slowly walked toward him, clutching her husband's arm with every step. "Well," she said, when she came to a stop in front of them, "that was probably the most embarrassing moment of my life."

Cole gave her his best smile. "Don't be embarrassed. Your kids and grandkids are going to love that story for generations to come."

She returned his smile, but it looked shaky.

He wondered if she was in pain.

"I was rushing over here to say that I didn't know who you were until just a few minutes ago. And now that I know who you are, I was hoping you would play me a song!"

Shucks. He didn't want to do that. He didn't want to be the center of attention at a wedding where he didn't know anyone.

Lettie tried to come to his rescue. "Uh ... he didn't bring his guitar."

"No problem! This is Tennessee." She turned to face her friends and family. "Does anyone have a guitar with them?"

Three people raised their hands, and Cole's stomach flipped.

She turned back to him with an expectant smile.

"I'd be honored, ma'am."

12

Lettie was speechless. That didn't happen often, but here it was. She couldn't tell whether Cole was happy about the situation. If he wasn't, he was doing a good job of faking it. But, she figured, he probably had to fake a lot of things in his career. She knew her mother sure had. Whether or not he was happy, Lettie sure wasn't. First of all, how presumptuous of Valerie! Sure, it was her wedding day, but that didn't mean complete strangers had to do her bidding, and you just don't go around asking professionals to perform for free. Second, Lettie *hated this!* She was so angry she feared her blood was boiling. For a few hours, she'd forgotten Cole was a country star. He'd just been a nice man. He'd just been her friend. But it was kind of hard to ignore his line of work now.

The deejay had a microphone, but no stand, so people were scrambling to find a way to prop the mic in front of Cole's mouth. One scantily clad woman with a tan that just had to be fake offered to stand in front of him and hold it, but, thank the heavens, someone else had declared how absurd that was.

The guitar that materialized out of someone's trunk looked old enough to be a relic. Cole busied himself tuning it, but it appeared to be an uncompliant instrument. He finally either got it in tune or gave up trying and then managed to convince all the busybodies that he didn't need a microphone. Then he turned to face the crowd, gave them a huge smile Lettie was beginning to understand was his stage smile, and said, "Hi, I'm Cole Washburne, and I'm the guest of the bride's cousin, Lettie." He dramatically swept his arm toward Lettie, and her cheeks grew hot. "That's my girlfriend, folks. Isn't she beautiful?" He held his grin and gazed at her, and heavens to Betsy, didn't it seem like he meant every word! She was so hot she thought she might melt. Turn into a puddle right there in that folding metal chair. She tried to smile, but she felt incredibly conspicuous and uncomfortable. No one was ever going to believe she hated country music ever again. And it was very important to her that people who knew her knew that fact to be true. Very important.

Cole returned his gorgeous gaze to the adoring audience. Everyone with a cell phone was pointing it at Cole. He scanned the room and found the bride. Then he tried to tip his hat to her—except he wasn't wearing a hat. He seemed to realize this midstream and let out an awkward chuckle. Lettie noticed then how incredibly different he looked up there without his hat. She liked it. "Did you have any song in mind?" he asked her.

Valerie chewed her lip for a second, and then inspiration dawned on her face. "Oh, yes, please! Play 'You Make It Easy.'"

Cole's smile flickered but then returned to full strength. "That's not my song."

Some of the crowd laughed.

Cole didn't look angry, but Lettie was angry enough for both of them. She was about to go claw her cousin's eyes out. As if the anger triggered something in her brain, her eyes drifted to Jason. He was staring directly at her. She quickly looked back to Cole, who was still smiling. Good grief, he was going to have facial arthritis one day.

The bride giggled. "That's okay! Play it anyway!"

The smile held on, but something changed in Cole's eyes.

That a boy. Tell her where to stick it!

"Sorry, I don't know the song." He paused, as if unsure how to proceed. "Do you want to hear one of mine?"

Valerie's lips moved, but no sound came out. She was dumbfounded. Good. Lettie liked her quiet.

"How about 'I Can See the Future'?" Cole tried. "Some of y'all have probably heard it on the radio."

The girl with the super-tan began to cheer. "Yah! I love that song!"

Cole looked relieved and nodded to her. "Great. Me too. All right, let's give her a rip." And he began to play.

"Wait!" the groom called out.

Cole stopped strumming.

Lettie couldn't take it anymore. She stood up abruptly, her chair making a loud screech on the floor. She opened her mouth to jump to Cole's defense, to tell them all off, but then she felt Jason's eyes on her, and she froze, even though most of the eyes in the room, including Cole's, were on her. Her whole body went cold, and no words came. So she sat back down and hung her head, wishing she had remembered to bring her invisibility cloak.

The groom continued, "Can you just wait till I find the photographer? He should film this! Hang on! I'll be right back!"

Lettie put her head in her hands. This just kept getting worse. As if the hundred filming cell phones weren't coverage enough. This would be all over YouTube within the hour.

13

Cole couldn't remember the last time he'd been so irritated. With all his might, he focused on not letting it show. Just one song, and then he'd get out of there—somehow. It was clear that Lettie was mortified, and he ached to comfort her. None of this was her fault; it sort of came with the territory. He was a middle-of-the-road artist. If he hadn't had any success, no one would have wanted him to play. If "You Make It Easy" really were his song, no one would have dared ask him to play it. So he waited, awkwardly, while the groom fetched the photographer.

Finally, they reappeared, and without waiting for permission Cole began to strum again. Then as he began to sing, his eyes drifted around the room. He'd been trained to make eye contact with his listeners, and he tried to do so, but he quickly became distracted by Jason getting up from his chair. The man wore an evil expression that Cole wanted to wipe right off his face. Cole panicked a little that he was going to approach Lettie, but he didn't. He went in the other direction, and Cole tried to stop watching him as he wound up for the chorus.

When he hit those first few notes, as expected, recognition dawned on some of the faces, and some of the people began smiling and tapping their toes. But not the people in Jason's vicinity. They were all whispering amongst themselves—loudly. Jason gave him a smug smile and returned to his seat.

Cole was certainly distracted, but no one would be able to tell. He could perform this song in his sleep. The people Jason spoke to were *not* smiling or tapping their toes. Their grins had been replaced with grimaces, and a few of the older women were doing their best to scold him with their eyes. *What on earth?* And then he saw it—whatever *it* was—travel across the room in a slow wave. Each person leaned to someone close to them and, via a quick, hushed word, spread the grimace to their neighbor. One by one, the feet stopped tapping. Cole's neck got hot around his collar, and he looked at Jason, who now wore an innocent-as-a-lamb expression. He put both his hands in front of him, palms up, and shrugged at Cole. Oh wow, this guy was something else.

Cole finished the song with a flourish, gave everyone another smile, and said "Thank you." No one applauded. The room was silent. He looked at Lettie, whose brow was furrowed in confusion. He strode toward the center of the room and returned the guitar to its owner, who took it and said, "You should be ashamed of yourself." The people around him nodded solemnly.

"I beg your pardon?"

A woman behind the guitar owner piped up. "We just heard about your affair. Loretta deserves better."

Cole barked out a laugh. "Loretta? She deserves better? Y'all care about Loretta all of a sudden?" He shook his head and turned toward Lettie. He strode as fast as he could without running, and she stood up before he got there and reached for his hand.

"He didn't have an affair with anyone!" she cried. "Those are just tabloid rumors, and you all are so gullible you'll believe any trash Jason spews." She whirled and yanked Cole out through the back door.

The heat assaulted them, but it felt so good to be outside. "Well, no good deed goes unpunished," he said, trying to make light of the situation.

Lettie stopped walking. She put her face in her hands, and her shoulders started shaking.

He turned and embraced her, even though it was really too hot for hugging. "There, there. Don't worry about it. It's okay."

She looked up at him and sniffed. "You saw their faces. They think I'm crazy. They don't even know who Jason is. He's going to spin this to make me sound paranoid again. But he was the one who spread the rumor! I saw him! I *saw* him do it!"

He stepped back and put his hands on her shoulders, amused that she wasn't upset about *his trauma* at all. "I know. I saw it too. And who cares what those people think? If you never saw any of them ever again, would you miss them?"

She smiled through her tears. "I guess not."

He turned toward the truck, but kept one arm around her shoulders. He gave her a little squeeze, pulling her into him, and kissed her on the side of the head. "Okay then. Let's just call this a bust and move on with our lives."

She giggled and nodded. "You're right."

"Come on, let's get in the truck. It has air conditioning." He unlocked and opened the door for her.

Instead of climbing in, she turned to face him. "Do you think we could go for ice cream? Or did you eat too many deviled eggs?"

14

Cole said he knew the perfect spot, and Lettie was inclined to trust his ice cream judgment. Still, once she had ice cream on the brain, it was a long ride back to Nashville. She really should have eaten some of that reception food.

"So that was pretty funny when Valerie fell on her face, huh?" She looked at him and smiled.

"Oh, stop it. I know you don't really wish her any harm. That looked like it hurt."

"Pft! You're such a softy."

"Don't I know it. So, it seems you didn't really want to be at the wedding at all. Why'd you go?"

She blew some stray hairs off her forehead. "That's an excellent question. I guess I just felt like I was supposed to."

"Ah, well, it was kind of you to go."

"Thanks."

They rode along in comfortable silence, and Lettie enjoyed the scenery. She felt really comfortable with Cole. It was too bad that he was a singer. Maybe they could have had something, that is, if Mr. Conventional could put up with as many tattoos as she had. She looked at him. "Do you have any ink?"

He gave her a quick glance and laughed. "What? Where did that come from?"

She shrugged. "Just trying to make conversation."

He tightened his grip on the wheel and shook his head. "I assume you mean tattoos, and you're not asking to borrow a ballpoint pen?"

She giggled. "That would be an accurate assumption."

"Well, then, no, I don't have any *ink*. Is that a problem?"

"No, I don't require my fake boyfriends to have tattoos," she said and then instantly regretted it when she saw him flinch. Shoot. Why had she said that? Sure, he *was* her fake boyfriend, but he obviously didn't like being called that. After ice cream, it was probably time for a fake breakup—

"Why do you have *so many*?" he interrupted her thoughts.

She thought about that for a second. "I'm not sure. I like tattoos, but they're also kind of addictive. Plus, I dated a tattoo artist for a while, so I could get them for cheap."

He glanced at her. "So you have your ex's art all over you."

She smirked. He had a point. "I didn't think about that at the time, but it's okay. We parted amicably. It's not like I let Jason tattoo me."

He glanced at her arm. "Let's not talk about him. Tell me what's with all the birds."

She looked down at her sparrows, even though of course she knew what he was talking about. "You know that Bible verse about God watching out for the sparrows? I always liked that, so I had some sparrows put on. It was one of the first tats I got."

"You're religious?" He couldn't have sounded more stunned.

"Not really, but I believe in God, of course."

"Of course. So you should go to church with me tomorrow."

She looked at him quickly. *What?* "I'm not really much of a churchgoer."

"I assumed so, but I *am*, and if you're my girlfriend, wouldn't you be in church with me?"

So much for the post-ice cream breakup. He was planning to extend this charade at least through tomorrow. "Maybe."

"Maybe?"

"Maybe. That's all I can commit to right now." She tipped her head back on the headrest. "I'm exhausted."

"I'm sure you are. That was quite an adventure we just had."

She didn't know why, but this struck her as funny, and she began to giggle. And then once she started, she couldn't stop. She was so tired, she was punchy.

"You have the cutest giggle."

Huh? What did *that* mean? That was kind of a flirtatious thing to say, wasn't it? But before she could finish analyzing it, he asked, "Do you think they've posted my impromptu wedding performance on YouTube yet?"

"I dunno. Want me to check?"

"If you want."

She could tell that he wanted her to, so she opened her YouTube app. "I have no idea how to find it."

"Me neither. YouTube is like the Wild West of the Internet."

She giggled again. Good grief, she had to get a grip. "No, that's Twitter."

"Oh, I wouldn't know. I don't tweet."

"Really? Twitter is awesome." She spent too much time on Twitter herself. "I'm surprised they don't make you do it. All the stars are tweeting."

"Oh, I have a Twitter account, but I don't even know the password. Someone else is tweeting for me."

Yikes. That would not sit well with her. She typed in his name and a zillion videos came up. She set the filter to "today" and then three of them popped right up. "Wowsa, not as hard as I thought. Yep, they've uploaded." One of them was titled, "Ironic Adulterer Sings at Wedding." Well, she didn't need to tell him about that one. The other two just had his name, and one of them was posted by the groom. She clicked on that one, and the sound of his voice filled the cab.

"Not bad for a hack," he said.

"You were very gracious to perform for them."

"I don't know as it was grace so much as I didn't have any other options. I would have been a jerk if I'd said no. But I sure regretted it when I realized I wasn't wearing my hat. I felt naked up there." He chuckled.

"You look good without your hat."

He gave her a sideways glance that crossed the border into flirtation. "Aw, shucks. You just don't like cowboy hats."

"I have nothing against cowboy hats." She just hated country singers who wore them when they had nothing to do with cows. "Are you a cowboy?"

"Not anymore, I hope."

"Oh? So, you were one once?"

"Yep. I grew up on a ranch. It's a beautiful life, but it's a lot of hard work."

So then no, she didn't mind the cowboy hat at all. "At least my brother wasn't at the wedding. Count our blessings, I guess."

"I thought he would be there."

"Me too."

"I wonder why he wasn't."

"No idea. Except that he hates weddings ... and family ... and people in general."

"There it is," he said, pointing with his chin.

If the fullness of the parking lot was any indication, the ice cream here would be every bit as delicious as Cole had promised. He pulled into the parking lot, drove around looking for a spot, didn't find one, and then pulled back out onto the road and parked on the shoulder. Then he rushed around to help her out of the truck, a gesture she was getting used to. Without thinking, she slid her hand into his, and he looked down in surprise at their intertwined fingers. Oops, but oh well—too late to back out now.

They strode hand in hand to the window. "Do you know what you want?" he asked.

"Not yet, but it seems I have plenty of time to decide." The line was at least a mile long.

"Do you want to skip it? We don't have to wait."

"Oh, no, no, I wasn't complaining. Are you kidding? This is the best part of the date." Wait, what? Why had she used the word date? Was she forgetting that all of this was make believe? She would do well to remind herself of that fact. Maybe she should put a rubber band around her wrist and snap herself every time she said or did something stupid. Or maybe she should just end the farce and set the poor cowboy free. She studied the many options on the menu. "You're buying, right?"

"Of course. A gentleman always buys."

The feminist in her should have argued, but she didn't want to pay.

It was finally their turn. He stepped up to the window. "Good evening, ma'am. Could I please get a triple scoop of vanilla?"

Of course.

He looked at her and gestured toward the window.

"Hi. Could I get a bowl of double dark chocolate frozen yogurt with lemon curd on top?"

Cole snorted as he let go of her hand. At first, she thought he dropped her hand out of disgust at her order, but then she realized he was just reaching for his wallet. "That is the weirdest ice cream order in the history of ice cream orders." It would have offended her, but he was smiling like he'd won the lottery.

15

When Cole walked her to the door this time, he was in an inexplicably good mood. *Maybe it's a sugar buzz.* The truth was, he didn't want to walk away from her. The night was young. Maybe she wanted to hang out? He tried to think of a reason why they would need to hang out together.

As they reached the door, she turned and daintily covered a huge yawn, which, to his eyes, looked manufactured. "I am sooo tired!"

Hm. Sugar must have a markedly different effect on her.

"Okay, then, I'll get out of your hair."

He thought her cheeks got pinker, but he couldn't be sure. *Do I kiss her? Do I not kiss her? She's not really my girlfriend? But she is a girl, and I do want to kiss her.*

"Okay, then, good night," she said, calling attention to the awkward pause he'd created.

"Right. Good night." He turned to go, and with every step, he wanted to turn back around, take her in his arms and kiss her. But he didn't. He just kept walking, until he was safe inside the cab of his truck.

Now what? *I guess I'll just go home. Maybe I've had enough excitement for one night.* So that's what he did. And he was grateful that his roommates weren't there. He lay down on the couch and turned on *Longmire*. He'd seen all the episodes, but he still loved to watch them. He loved Nashville, and it was his home now, but that didn't mean he didn't miss Wyoming.

Five minutes later, he realized he was drifting off to sleep. *Man, I guess I was tired too,* he thought, and then let himself go. He dreamed that he woke up and found Natalie in his living room. He was happy to see her, but was also really, *really* angry with her. "How could you do this to me?" he asked her, but she didn't respond. In the dream, he got up to go to the bathroom, and when he looked into the mirror, he saw that his hair was several different shades of pink.

This startled him, and he woke up to a cool, dark living room and a message on the television screen that read, "Are you still watching Longmire?" Annoyed, he clicked "yes" and then looked at his phone to see what time it was.

He had a text message from Lettie: "Can you come over?"

He sat up straighter. Shoot, she'd sent it an hour ago.

"Sorry, I was asleep. Sure, I'll be right there."

"Hurry."

Something in his gut twisted. What was going on? He got up and grabbed his truck keys as he swiped, "Is everything okay?"

"I think so."

What on earth did that mean?

He had run halfway down the walk when he realized he hadn't shut the door. That wouldn't do, so he turned and hustled back to lock up. Then he trotted to the truck, trying to stay calm. *This is probably nothing. She's probably just bored.* Except that he didn't think Lettie would invite him over because she was *bored.*

He hurried across town, and it took far longer than he thought it would. He eyed the phone on the seat beside him. He so wanted to text her that he was on his way, but he didn't want to pull over to do so, and he didn't want to crash and die either. So he just focused on the driving and only ran one red light in the name of being the white knight.

Finally, he arrived, and tried to play it cool while he rushed from his truck to her front door. He had the oddest sensation that someone was watching him. He looked around the quiet, still neighborhood, but didn't see anyone. He went inside and knocked on her door, which she opened immediately. She threw her arms around his neck and pulled him inside. "Oh, thank you!" She was wearing a silky black bathrobe that almost made him blush.

He was relieved to see she was wearing old sweats under it. "What's going on?"

"I'm not sure." She sat on the couch, and he followed suit. "But my roommate's at her boyfriend's, and Jason posted 'I'm outside' on my Facebook—"

"He did what?" Cole jumped up to look out the window, but she had every blind closed and every curtain drawn.

"No, don't," she said and pulled him back down to sit beside her. "That's exactly what he wants is for us to freak out. But I thought, since you are my serious boyfriend and all, that it didn't make sense for you not to be here."

Oh. So that's all she wanted. She didn't want his protection or his company. She just wanted to keep up appearances. He couldn't believe how disappointed this knowledge left him.

"Do you know if he's really out there?"

She nodded. "He deleted the Facebook post seconds after I'd seen it, but then I heard scratching outside the window."

"Scratching? Are you serious?" The guy was a nut!

"Yes, but really, he's harmless. Don't worry. Just sit here with me. Let's watch television really loud. He'll probably go away if you're—"

"Harmless? He's not harmless! We should call the cops!"

"And tell them what?" she practically screeched. "This is how he operates! I have nothing to tell them! I don't have the Facebook post, and all I have are scratching sounds that they'll say are mice in the walls."

Cole looked around the dark room, lit only by a collection of lava lamps in the corner. "*Do* you have mice in the walls?"

She giggled. "Yes, but I promise you, this wasn't them."

He rested his fingers on her arm. "I know. I believe you. All right then. I still think we should call the police, but if you don't want to, let's watch television. Do you have any popcorn?"

"I do not. But I have Ho Hos."

"What?"

"You know, those little frosted cake rolls. They're my favorite."

"Uh ..." He didn't want to insult her, but did those even count as food? He thought he'd seen them in movies. He was certain he'd never eaten one.

Her face fell.

"I would *love* a Ho Ho," he said quickly.

"Just one? They come in packages of two."

"Sure. I would love *two* Ho Hos." Would he even be able to choke them down?

She giggled and jumped up to fetch the strange snacks, and he found himself straining to listen to outdoor noises, but he couldn't hear anything.

She returned in a rush, with her robe riding her wake, looking a little like a superhero. She sat down beside him and handed him a cellophane package before ripping into hers. "Okay, what are we watching?"

"How about *Longmire*?" He gingerly opened his package.

"Never seen it."

"You're kidding." He was suddenly so excited to introduce her to Walt. And now that he thought about it, she did remind him a little of Victoria. He bit into the Ho Ho gingerly as he pressed play. He chewed slowly, a little afraid of what was about to happen in his mouth, but it wasn't so bad. Sort of like eating air. "Aren't these just Swiss Rolls?"

She glowered at him. "No. They're *Ho Hos*. Far superior to Swiss Rolls." She shoved an entire Ho Ho into her mouth.

He laughed so suddenly that he almost lost some of his own half-chewed Ho Ho. He hurried to swallow and then wiped his mouth. "Wow, you take your Ho Hos seriously."

She gave him a big smile. She had tiny pieces of chocolate on her bottom lip. "Yes, yes, I do." Once again, the sugar acted as a sedative, and before the pilot was over, she had fallen asleep with her head resting lightly on his shoulder. He watched two more episodes on low volume, but never heard a noise outside. He figured that *if* Jason had been there, he was gone now. *Had* he been there? Of course he had. Lettie wouldn't have imagined all that.

Either way, he didn't know what to do. Should he leave? Should he move to a chair and cover her up with a blanket? Or should he stay right where he was and keep watching television? He opted for the latter and eventually nodded off to the sound of rifle fire.

16

Lettie woke up with cold toes and a stiff neck. Why was she on the couch? Then it all came flooding back, and she looked around frantically for Cole. Had he left? Without saying anything? Then she heard water running in the bathroom. She sure hoped that was him.

It was. He opened the door and smiled at her. "Good morning, sleepyhead."

"Morning," she said, feeling sheepish all of a sudden. "You didn't have to sleep over. That wasn't my intention."

"I know, but it seemed like a good idea. I'm glad we made it through the night without any other creepy occurrences."

"You didn't hear anything after I fell asleep?"

He shook his head. "Not a peep."

"He was here. I swear."

"I know, I know," he said, crossing the room quickly. He sat down and put his hand over hers. "I believe you."

She couldn't believe it. He was the first person to believe her about Jason—ever. And he didn't have as much evidence as some of the others had had. She was profoundly grateful, but she didn't know how to tell him that. "Well, it's daylight now, so I should be safe. He doesn't usually skulk around in the light."

He leaned back on the sofa. "I've got a great idea."

"Oh yeah?"

"Yeah. Let's go to church!"

"Church?" She didn't want to go to church. "How about breakfast?"

He picked up his phone. "I don't think we have time for breakfast before church. But I can take you to brunch after church?"

She smirked. She wouldn't have thought Cole would use the word "brunch." She didn't know what to say. She didn't want to disappoint him, but she really didn't want to go sit in a pew and be talked at. Suddenly, she realized she must look a fright. She self-consciously smoothed out her hair and was suddenly desperate to brush her teeth. She jumped up and made a beeline for the bathroom. "Be right back," she said on her way, and then shut the door faster and louder than she'd meant to. *Oops.* She did some basic primping, looked in the mirror, and didn't feel any better. Why was she suddenly so worried about how she looked? She edged out of the bathroom. "Do we at least have time for some coffee and a Pop-Tart?"

He laughed at her. "You go ahead. I could just go for some orange juice, if you have any."

She didn't, but she thought her roommate probably did. She could borrow some of it. "Let me see what I can rustle up."

He kept talking about church as if it was a done deal, and before she knew it, she found herself wearing semi-normal clothes and sitting in the cab of his truck. "Do you go to church alone usually?"

"I did at first. I promised my mom it was one of the first things I'd do when I got to Nashville. Otherwise, I'm not sure she would have let go of me and let me get in the truck. But now I know lots of people there. It's my manager's church. I didn't know that when I started going there, but I'm thinking maybe that helped me get him."

"Is he a big name in management?"

"Not really, but he's been doing it for years. I'm really happy with him."

"Is Shawn the only music person there?"

He looked at her, and his expression softened. "It's a good mixture of folks. No one will be talking about music. At least, I don't think they will be." He paused, and she could feel him gearing up to take the conversation deeper. "What happened with you and music? Did you used to sing?"

She scoffed, "Absolutely not."

"Then what is it?"

She was so *not* going there with him. She didn't even want to go there with herself. "I grew up in this city. It wears on you. I've seen what happens to people who worship in the church of country music."

"Well, this is just an ordinary church, and don't worry, I'll protect you."

"Speaking of protection, thank you so much for last night." She was grateful for the opportunity to take the conversation in a different direction.

"Don't mention it."

She got nervous when she saw how many cars were in the church parking lot. "Maybe this isn't such a good idea. I haven't been to church in years."

He turned off the engine and hopped out of the truck. "If that's the case, then this is a great idea." She watched him hurry around the front of his truck and open the door for her. She tried to will herself to relax as she accepted his hand. For two people who weren't dating, they spent an awful lot of time holding hands. But were they dating? Was this turning into something? If so, she had to nip it in the bud. No matter how handsome or kind or sweet he was, he was still a musician. He led her inside. She politely nodded to anyone who looked at her and then slid into a pew beside him. Wow—butt in the pew two days in a row. How had her life taken such a strange turn?

A man went up front to welcome them all, and then a band started to play. She rolled her eyes at the introductory guitar riff, but she kept her commentary to herself. The lyrics were projected on a giant screen, and she read along as the congregation started to sing. She didn't know the song, but even if she did, she wasn't about to sing. She hadn't sung so much as a Christmas carol since she was little.

Cole's voice lifted above their neighbors', and she found its sound incredibly soothing. The man really could sing. She allowed herself to enjoy his voice, the joyful lyrics, and the ambiance—and a wonderful sense of peace washed over her, so much so that when the music ended, and everyone sat down, she was sad that it was over.

17

On Monday morning Cole had a meeting with his label, Evelyn Records. Everyone there had always been kind to him, but he still felt he was in over his head every time he walked through the door. He couldn't believe how lucky he'd been to get signed by them. They were one of the smaller labels in town. Last he knew, they only had ten artists, but there wasn't a dud in the bunch. The label had been founded by the great Branch Bronson, one of Cole's biggest heroes. As far as he could tell, Branch was pretty hands off with the management of the label, but the CEO, as well as the A&R guy, knew what they were doing. Everyone they had signed was currently on the charts, Cole included.

Today they were meeting to finalize the launch date for his debut album, and, he assumed, to schedule the launch party. As he sat in the futuristic-looking conference room, he wondered if Lettie would go to the launch party with him. Probably not. That wasn't really her thing.

Louis Leypold entered the room, with Cole's manager trailing behind. A woman Cole didn't know followed them in. He stood to offer his hand, which Louis took.

"Thanks for coming in, Cole. Have a seat. This is Angela, one of my administrative assistants. She's going to be helping us with the scheduling." That explained the open laptop she had carried into the room. "Let's get right down to business. Cole, we are thrilled with how well your single is doing."

Cole smiled. No one was as thrilled as he was.

"And I think it's crucial to choose the next single wisely. I'd like to ride this momentum. I know you wanted to release one of your ballads, but I think we should try to mimic the sound of this first single. We'll show your range eventually, but for now, let's stick with what we know works."

Angela's fingers flew across the keyboard. Cole wondered what on earth she was typing. They hadn't really decided anything yet.

Cole nodded. "Okay." He loved all the songs on his album, so didn't care which one they released. He was grateful that he hadn't known Natalie when he wrote those songs, so none of them were about her.

"Okay?" Louis said and looked at Shawn with eyebrows raised. "That was easy!"

Shawn leaned back in his swivel chair and smiled like a proud papa. "Cole is pretty easy to get along with."

"Huh," Louis said, "that's great. We don't get a lot of that around here. You know, artists are artists." He laughed at his own words.

Cole didn't care about the details. As long as he was on the radio.

"So," Louis continued, "we're looking at the fifteenth for your official launch date."

"Really?" This was great news.

"Yep. It's ready to go, so let's get it out there. We're still looking for a date for the launch party, as we're waiting for a few other events to be scheduled. We don't want to be competing for attendees. Which brings me to the big news. I know we had planned to send you out on tour with The Belles, but a spot has just opened up on Branch's tour, and he wants you to fill it.

Cole almost fell out of his chair. "Seriously?"

Louis laughed. "Seriously. Branch likes your music, but he also likes your image. Now, the tour has already started. Blayze has been opening for him, but he's had to drop off the tour."

Cole had heard the rumors. Blayze was a handful. No wonder Branch liked Cole's image. It was the exact opposite of Blayze's image—which was whiskey and women. Cole wondered why Evelyn had ever signed him in the first place. "Okay, so I've missed a few shows."

"You have. And you're missing one tonight. How fast do you think you can get on the bus?"

"Uh ... I can get on the bus right now." An image of Lettie flashed through his mind. He tried to ignore it.

Louis laughed again. "That's the spirit! Well, it will take us a few days to get your band together. It will be small, and we've got some musicians in mind, but we've got to finalize some details. How about Friday?"

"*This* Friday?" But what about Lettie's stupid ex? He would have to make sure she had someone else to call in case he came creeping around.

"Yeah. Does that work for you?"

"Yes!" Cole said, with a touch more enthusiasm than he felt. "That's perfect."

"Great!" Louis said and slapped the table.

"Great," Shawn echoed. Then, as if reading Cole's mind, "How's Lettie doing?"

"She's great," Cole said too quickly.

"Good. It was good to see her in church with you yesterday."

"Yes, it was good to have her there." The atmosphere turned awkward, and Cole didn't really understand why.

"All right," Louis said, looking at Angela. "So, we'll get ready for the tour, and we're still looking for a party date, but it will be right around your launch date, if not on it." He looked at Cole. "We'll fly you back for it, of course."

Cole nodded. He didn't really care about logistics.

"So, as for the next single, let's release 'Pig Scramble.'"

"Sounds good."

"My, you *are* easy to get along with. I appreciate that." Louis looked at Angela. "Do we have everything we need?"

She nodded, her fingers still flying.

Louis stood, leaned over the table, and extended his hand. "Always a pleasure, Cole. Keep up the good work." He shook Cole's hand as he looked at Shawn. "Let me know if you need anything."

The meeting ended, and much to his relief, no one had mentioned the tabloid scandal. Either they hadn't heard about it, which he found doubtful, they didn't care, which he found even more doubtful, or they had dismissed it as false. Whatever the reason, he was grateful he hadn't had to discuss it.

He thanked Shawn and then headed out of the building, still reeling from the news. On tour with Branch Bronson. The opportunity of a lifetime. A career making moment. He was beyond thrilled. So then why couldn't he stop thinking about Lettie?

18

Lettie could hardly believe it when she looked up to see Cole coming into her bar. They had only just opened, and only a few hard-core regulars were there, working on their first beers. At the sight of him, a warmth filled her head and then spread down through her body all the way to her toes. She couldn't believe it. She had a crush on the cowboy. *Oh well, a crush can be harmless.* She gave him a quick smile and then went behind the bar. He followed her and slid onto a stool.

"Can I get you anything?"

"Do you guys serve food?"

She shook her head. "Just pretzels. Sorry."

"Shucks, I was hoping for some Ho Hos."

She giggled. That did sound good to her, but, alas, no Ho Hos in sight. "How about something to drink?"

"Sure. Orange juice then—on the rocks."

She laughed. "Are you serious?"

"Deadly."

"Okay. Coming right up." She turned to open the fridge and noticed her hand was shaking. She had to get a grip. She found the orange juice, a moderately clean glass, and some ice, and then she poured him his drink. She slid it down the bar to him, just like they do in the movies, but unlike what happens in the movies, when it hit his hand, it sloshed all over it and his sleeve. Oops.

"Could I get a napkin, ma'am?"

She giggled and handed him a stack of napkins. "In case you want a refill. So, what brings you to this part of town? Don't you country stars have too full of a schedule to be drinking in the middle of the day?"

"Actually, I came because I have some news."

"Oh?" Her heart rate picked up. She didn't know why. What news of Cole's could possibly affect her?

"Yeah. I already told my mom and my sister, and now I'm telling you! Branch Bronson wants me on his tour. I leave Friday." Her stomach sank, and he held up a hand as if to stall the sinking. "Don't worry, I talked to a buddy of mine. He's really cool, an older songwriter I go to church with. But he's tough and he's been around the block a time or two. He's married with kids, so there won't be any creepiness—"

"What are you talking about?"

He leaned toward her and lowered his voice. "I didn't just want to leave you hanging with the Jason situation." He reached into his pocket as he was talking and pulled out a slip of paper. "This is his number. He said to just give him a call anytime anything happens, or if you get freaked out."

What the heck? Without unfolding the piece of paper, she firmly and quickly slid it back across the bar toward him. "I don't need some stranger's phone number. I can take care of myself."

He sat up straight. "I know you can. But that guy is a criminal. You don't want to mess around with that. And if you won't call the cops—"

"I'm not calling the cops because I can take care of myself." She knew she was contradicting herself. Two nights ago she had texted him in a crying panic, asking for his help and now here she was pretending to be too tough to need it. She wished she'd never invited him over. Why had she done that? "I know you probably think you're helping, but you're not. Thanks for trying, though. So, I suppose we should break up?"

He blinked like he'd been slapped. "I don't know? Have you heard from your brother?"

"I have, actually. I texted him and asked why he didn't go to the wedding."

Cole took a long drink of his orange juice and set the almost empty glass down on a napkin. "And? What did he say?"

"He said he had to work." She didn't know if she should elaborate.

There was a pregnant pause. Then, "What are you not telling me?"

She took a deep breath. Might as well pull the Band-Aid off in one quick yank. "He was still following your ... ex. He said he caught her with someone else." She paused and waited for the outcry. But there wasn't one.

Surprise barely registered on his face. "Really?" If he was crushed, he was hiding it well.

She put her elbows on the bar and leaned on them. Now that she was closer to him, she could smell the cedar again. She was going to miss that scent. Would have to get some cedar shavings for her apartment. *That probably wouldn't have the same effect.* "He specifically said that he figured you were off the hook. He said he wasn't convinced that nothing was going on, because he saw your hat hanging at her table, but he said he doubted she was having more than one affair at a time."

Cole looked down and studied his glass.

She tried to think of something else to say, something that would distract him from whatever he was feeling, whether it was embarrassment or hurt. She couldn't read him, but whatever he was feeling, it was evident he wasn't enjoying it. But she couldn't think of a single helpful word.

Without looking up, he asked, "How did he know it was my hat?"

She snickered, and then he did look up at her, and his eyes seemed to be searching her soul. "He didn't know, until he came back inside and saw you wearing it, you big goof."

Cole rubbed his jaw. "Oh yeah ... *that*. Obviously, I'm not very good at sneaking around."

She wanted to touch him. She didn't, though. "Well, you'll never have to do it again. I think you learned your lesson, right?"

He nodded vigorously. "You got that right. Someday, when the heat has long since died down, I will get a song out of being tricked into an affair. But I'm not ready to write it yet."

"You write all your own songs?"

He looked happy at her interest. "I thought I would, but my label wanted me to have some different sounds on my record, so they had me listen to a couple hundred demos and find a few songs that weren't my own. In fact, my next single is going to be called 'Pig Scramble.'" He chuckled. "And I've never even been to a pig scramble."

"Me neither."

"Lettie," he started, his voice thick with emotion, "I'm really glad to have met you. And I'm really grateful to you for helping me out of that scrape. You're right. I guess our fake relationship should have a fake breakup, but I'd like to be friends with you."

These were kind words, so why were they making her angry? "Oh, you say that now. But you're on the rise. Soon you'll forget all about little ole me."

He furrowed his handsome brow. "That's not true."

"You'll see." She stood up straight, grabbed the bar towel, and started wiping the freshly cleaned bar. Her eyes felt hot, and she kept them trained on the towel.

He put his hand over hers. "Fine. I'll just have to prove you wrong." He moved his hand, and her skin felt lonely at its absence. He reached for his wallet. "I guess I'll get out of your hair."

She held up a hand. "This one's on the house. You take good care of yourself, Cole. You're a good man. Don't let the business ruin that goodness."

He gave her a grave look. "I won't." She thought he was done talking, but then he added, "I don't think this business ruins people, Lettie."

"You'll see about that too." She knew she was being depressing and forced a smile. "Congrats about Branch Bronson, though. Even I know who he is."

Cole nodded without returning her smile. "I think everybody does." He stared at her, and she wondered when he was going to leave. Part of her was in a hurry for that to happen, but part of her didn't want that to ever happen. "Can I get a hug?" he asked, his voice thick again. Oh boy. She shouldn't hug him, but it would be so rude to say no. She came around the bar and closed the gap between them. He wrapped his big arms around her, and she breathed in his scent as she slid one arm around his waist. He kissed her on top of the head. "It's been a pleasure, Loretta. Call or text me anytime." And then he turned and walked out of her bar and out of her life.

19

On Wednesday morning, Cole got to meet his band for the first time. He'd worked with some awesome musicians in the studio, but alas, none of them were going to be on the road with him. He wasn't surprised, but that didn't stop him from being a little disappointed. He'd bonded with them, and they'd made his songs sound so good.

But his new band also seemed pretty talented, and everyone except the drummer seemed laid back and friendly. The drummer, whose name was Kermit, was a little grumpy. His clothes were really ripped up too, which either meant he lived with a big, mean cat, or he had a fashion sense similar to Lettie's. At the thought of her, Cole's chest tightened. He missed her. A lot. So he'd been trying not to think about her. He didn't need to be missing his fake ex-girlfriend, especially since she obviously wasn't missing him. She'd been downright rude when he'd gone to share his news, acting like she knew more about the music industry than he did, like she was some wise old sage who knew everything. What a crock. She didn't know anything. She was a waitress. *Server*, he corrected himself in his head. Whatever you called her gig, it had nothing to do with the music business.

"You ready to rehearse?" his new band leader, Harvey, asked, and Cole got the sense that it wasn't the first time the guy had asked.

"Yeah, yeah, let's go." Cole was excited. This was fun. He tried to focus on that as he got ready to sing the first line of "Pig Scramble." Sure, he'd picked this song, and sure, it was a good song, and sure, he thought it could be a hit, but he also thought maybe he'd be sick of it after thirty-one shows. That's how many concerts Branch Bronson had left on his tour. Thirty-one. That meant he would be gone from

Nashville for months. Gone from Lettie for months. He shook his head to clear it and tried to focus on the lyrics.

Harvey stopped playing his guitar and waved off the rest of the band.

Cole stopped singing and looked at him. "What's up?"

"What's up?" he repeated, sounding incredulous. "Where's your head, man? You're half a beat behind us. Do you want us to slow the tempo?"

Cole shook his head quickly. "No, sorry about that. I've just got a lot on my mind."

Harvey gave him a patronizing look. Harvey was old enough to be his father and had probably shared the stage with a few up-and-comers.

"Sorry, man, I'll get it."

"All right." Harvey turned toward the band. "Take it from the top."

And the pig scramble began again. Cole successfully blocked Lettie from his thought stream as he tried to put himself into the song, which was tough, as he'd never seen kids chase a pig around a pen. He vowed to watch some pig scrambles on YouTube before he performed this song in public. He stepped back from the microphone to allow the drummer to show off. He was a good drummer, so it was okay that he was a grouch. Smiling with sheer joy, Cole stepped back up to the microphone and started to sing again. This was so fun. Rehearsing with his own band, getting ready to go out on the road to open for the band that opened for Branch Bronson. This was the life he'd always dreamed of.

He saw Shawn walk in and nodded to him as he continued to sing. Shawn looked like he wasn't having any fun.

Cole finished the song and then walked to the edge of the stage. "Everything okay?"

"Finish up," Shawn said. "We can talk about it after."

A ball of lead formed in Cole's stomach. "It's okay. Let's talk about it now."

Shawn looked pained, but he trotted up onto the stage. "Well, good news, and bad news."

"All right. Good first."

"You've been invited to sing at the Opry."

Cole almost fell over. Could this day get any better? "Really? That's great! When?"

"Well, it's going to be tough to schedule with the tour, but we'll try to coordinate it with your launch party, so that you only have to come back to Nashville once."

"Great! Do I get to—"

"Now, for the not-so-great news. Branch heard about your incident."

Oh no. Cole waited for Shawn to elaborate. "And?"

"And he's concerned."

"Well, he shouldn't be. I'm not seeing that woman."

"I know, but you *were*—"

"Did you *tell* him that?" No way. He was sunk.

"I didn't tell him anything. I didn't talk to him directly. This is all through Louis. But I don't want to lie to the guy."

Cole didn't want to do that either. "Don't lie. We'll just tell him that I'm dating Lettie."

Shawn scowled. "I thought that was fake, and I thought you pretended to break up."

"I'll go un-break up with her." He'd spoken the words a little too fast, a little too easily. "Then you can just tell Branch that I'm seriously involved with a woman who's *not* married."

Shawn nodded thoughtfully. "If you want to go that route, but I'm not sure it's necessary. We could just tell him you're innocent and see how things shake out. I don't know if I want to encourage you to pretend to date a woman. What if *that* ever got out? It could be almost as embarrassing as the original rumor."

Cole massaged his jaw. "Shawn, the truth is ... maybe it's not so fake." He looked at him, trying to say with his eyes what he couldn't find the words to say.

Shawn chuckled. "Seriously?"

Cole nodded. "I mean, we did end things, but I do like her, so it wouldn't be so much of a stretch for me to try. I'm pretty confident she's not interested in me romantically, but I could try to be charming." He laughed, even though he hadn't been kidding.

Shawn stared at him, looking contemplative. "Cole, I know you pretty well by now, and I think I know what you want in life, what your goals are ... are you sure she fits in?"

Cole's chest tightened. He squared his shoulders. "What do you mean?"

Shawn took a small step back and put his hands in his pockets. "I just mean, I'm not sure she's the marrying type, or the maternal type. You told me you couldn't wait to settle down and have a family."

"I can't." Did Shawn have a point? Was Lettie too far out there for him? He tried, but he couldn't picture her behind the white picket fence.

Suddenly, Shawn slapped him on the shoulder. "You know what? Forget I said anything. Who am I to try and offer relationship advice? I've been divorced twice." He laughed a humorless laugh. "I should stick to the professional management and leave the personal management to you, Cole. Sorry about that." He ran a hand through his sparse hair. "All right, what do you want me to tell Louis?"

"That I am completely innocent." Cole thought for a few seconds. "I'm not seeing anyone at the moment, but marriage is sacred, and I am certainly not involved with a married woman."

Shawn nodded. "You don't think that woman would ever come forward, do you?"

How should he know? He'd thought she was a single woman in love with him. He didn't know anything about her. "I don't know, but I don't want to ever talk to her again, so I'm not going to ask."

Shawn nodded. "Okay then. I'll pass it on. Get back to your rehearsal. You sound great." He turned and walked away, humming the chorus of "Pig Scramble."

20

On Wednesday night, Lettie was in bed, almost asleep, when she heard her power go out. Rather, she heard the sudden absence of her ceiling fan and the hum of her refrigerator. She opened her eyes to see that the digital clock on her nightstand had gone black. *Did I forget to pay the light bill? Don't be silly. The power company doesn't turn people off in the middle of the night.* It was that thought that made her body break out in a cold sweat. Praying that the whole neighborhood would be dark, she lifted the blinds an inch and looked out the window to see that this was not the case. Instinctively, she pulled the covers up around her, but then realized she couldn't just stay in bed. Something was very wrong. She picked up the phone without even knowing who she was going to call until she was doing it.

"Cole? Can you please come over?" she whispered. "He's here."

"Yes! Be right there." He sounded groggy. "Keep the line open. I'm moving."

She wanted to talk to him, just to make some noise, but she was listening with all her might. She should go check to make sure the door was still locked. She crept toward her bedroom door, terror coursing through her. She peeked through the doorway, but didn't see anything. The streetlight outside would've cast a faint light across the living room, but she had the blinds shut and the curtains drawn.

"Lettie? Are you still there?"

"Yes," she whispered. "I'm going to turn on my flashlight, though, so I need to look at my phone." She lowered the phone from her ear, and, even though she was terrified about what she might see, she turned on the light, and then immediately shined it around the room. There was nothing.

"Lettie? I'm getting in the truck. Hang on."

She didn't answer. She didn't want to put her light source back up to her ear.

"Sweetie? You want to hang up and call the cops?"

Part of her noticed, and appreciated, him calling her sweetie. "No," she whispered. She crept to her roommate's bedroom. She knew she wasn't there, but wanted to check anyway. She touched the door, and it slowly swung open. Lettie shined the light on the bed, but it was neatly made up, as it had been since her roommate had met her latest flame.

"You want me to call them?"

She almost said yes. But, what would she tell them? She called them because the power went out? This was just like last time. He makes her look crazy, and then he skates away scot-free. She put the phone up to her ear. "No. Just hurry. Maybe he's gone—"

She heard something behind her and whirled around to stare into the darkness. But then, through her kitchen window, she saw movement. "I just saw him!"

"That's it. I'm calling the police."

"No! Please, don't!" She started to cry. She didn't want to. But the tears had a mind of their own. She crept closer to the window, half expecting him to jump through it and scare what was left of her wits right out of her.

"Okay, hang on, I'm almost there."

From her right, she heard whistling. As she strained to focus on it, it stopped, but then when she started breathing again, he started whistling again. *Oh my soul, he's whistling "Down-Home Dixie Time."* That was her mother's song. No one knew that song anymore. Except maybe her brother. Her mother had taken that song, along with all her others, to her grave. The whistling got louder, and her arms broke out in goosebumps. How did he know the tune so well? He'd never heard her mother sing it. The records. Those stupid demos. He must have some of them—or, knowing him, *all* of them. He was nothing if not thorough. The whistling stopped, and she sighed with relief. But then it started again, and he was back by the kitchen window. It sounded like he was right under it. This was a different song, though, not one of her mother's. This time he was whistling, "I Will Always Love You."

"I'm three blocks away. What's happening?"

"He's whistling."

"Whistling?"

"Yeah, he's whistling Dolly at me."

She knew she could fling open the back door and catch him in the act, expose him for the nutso he was. But she couldn't quite bring herself to move her feet. And so what if *she* caught him red-handed? She was the one who already knew he was crazy. She needed someone *else* to see the evidence.

Cole. Cole would see it. Cole believed her. As if her confidence in him summoned him, she heard a truck pull into the driveway. "Where is he?" Cole asked, scaring the snot out of her. She had forgotten he was still on the phone.

"Backyard."

21

Cole was *so* done with this lunacy. He killed his headlights even before he pulled into her driveway, and when she told him that Jason was in the backyard, he counted it a stroke of luck. It looked like a fence ran around the whole backyard, and he didn't think Jason was athletic enough to climb it. Maybe burrow under it like the snake he was, but not climb it. He turned off his interior light before he opened the door, so it wouldn't create any more light. He knew his engine had already announced his arrival, but he didn't need Jason seeing where he was and where he was going. He slid out of his truck, and staying low to the ground, headed for the backyard. Without hanging up, he slid the phone into his back pocket.

The backyard was darker than a skunk's funeral. And it was bigger than he'd imagined. Lots of hiding places. He looked around, straining his eyes. At first, there was nothing, but then he saw movement behind a shrub. Cole stood up straighter. "Come on out, ya yellow-belly. Face me like a man."

No movement and no response. Cole stepped closer to the bush. His desire to not let Jason get away far outweighed his desire to not fight the guy. As he got closer, he saw a shifting in the shadows. "Jason, I can see you. Stop hiding behind a plant."

And then, with more speed than Cole thought possible, Jason leapt out from behind the bush and sprinted for the wooden fence. Cole took off after him, but he was bigger and slower than the stalker, and Jason was gaining ground. Cole took personal offense to this. But at least he could see him now. And so he watched him run away, and then, just before Jason reached the fence, Cole watched him push off on one leg and leap, as if he was going up for a dunk. His right hand grabbed the top of the fence, but that was as close as he came to victory.

Jason's face smashed into the hard, wooden fence. "Ugh!" he cried out, sounding more offended than injured. The rest of his body followed his face. His chest slammed into the fence, and then his pelvis. The force of this ripped his hand free, and he tumbled to the ground in an embarrassing heap of creepy.

Cole was on him. He grabbed him, rolled him over to make sure it was, in fact, Jason, and when he did, he saw that the madman had a handgun tucked into his waistband. "Ah!" he cried out in surprise, as if he'd just seen a big hairy spider. He grabbed the gun by its handle, tossed it aside, and then rolled Jason back over and held him in place as he fished out his phone. Jason squirmed beneath him. "Oh, cut it out, ya big eel. You're not going anywhere." He held the phone up to his ear, a little embarrassed at how winded he was. "I got him. You're safe. If you've got a rope or extension cord or something, bring it outside, would ya?" Then he hung up and dialed 911.

He hadn't even finished relaying the address to the kind dispatcher when Lettie appeared holding a long purple strip of fleece.

"What's that?"

"It's the belt of my bathrobe."

He held his hand out for it, glad she hadn't brought the belt of the silky black bathrobe he'd encountered a few days ago. "That will work. Thanks." He tied Jason's hands behind his back, probably too tight, and then stood up and stretched his back, but before he knew what was happening, Lettie's arms were around him.

He hugged her back, and it felt so good to be back with her again, to be touching her, holding her.

"Thank you so much," she muttered into his chest. "You saved me."

What happened next was entirely an accident. He bent to kiss her on the top of the head, but at the same time, she looked up at him, and their lips met, awkwardly at first, but then she tilted her head to the side, and he slipped into heaven. No one had lips as soft as hers.

She ripped herself out of his arms, bringing her hand to her mouth. "I can't." And she turned and fled to the house.

"Well, I guess it's just you and me," Jason said, his mouth in the grass.

"Zip it."

Cole heard sirens, and they sounded *very* far away. He tried to be patient as he stood there in the dark thinking about that kiss.

Eventually, two police officers arrived, a man and a woman. They introduced themselves and then helped Jason to a standing position. Cole gave them a short recounting of events, and then the female officer read Jason his rights as she untied the purple belt from his wrists.

"Want to help me get the power back on?" the other officer asked, and Cole followed him into the basement, where they figured out that Jason had broken a basement window, climbed in, cut the power, and then, apparently, climbed out to whistle a Dolly Parton tune at his ex-girlfriend.

"He was a weird stalker," Cole said to the officer.

"Yes, but believe it or not, I've seen weirder."

"I believe it." Cole still didn't know *which* Dolly Parton tune Jason had serenaded her with. He thought probably "Here You Come Again" or "Old Flames."

When the men joined the women in the now well-lit living room, Lettie was explaining everything and the officer was rapidly scribbling notes. Cole peeked out the window and saw the cruiser in the yard with the lights flashing. Shoot, he'd missed watching Jason get shoved into the backseat.

Cole sat beside Lettie on the couch and put his arm around her. He wanted her to know that, awkward backyard adrenaline kiss or not, he was still there for her.

The female officer gave each of them her card and told them to call her if they thought of anything else or if they had any questions, and then she vanished.

22

Lettie didn't know what to say to her hero. Should she apologize for the kiss or pretend it had never happened? She wanted to just crawl back into bed, pull the covers up over her head, and go back to sleep. But he was in her apartment. On her couch. And she couldn't exactly kick him out after he'd ridden in on his white horse and rescued her.

"Why did he whistle at you?" Cole interrupted her thoughts with an obvious attempt to get some conversation started. Apparently, he had recognized the awkward silence too.

She closed her eyes and leaned her head back on the couch. "I'm not sure. He's not mentally well, and thank goodness someone other than me knows that now."

"I know ... but *whistling*? That's just so weird."

"He knows I hate music," she snapped, and instantly felt guilty for being short with him. She reached out and tentatively put her hand over his. "I'm sorry, I don't mean to be snippy. I'm a little out of sorts." She chuckled. "Even more out of sorts than usual. But I really don't know why he whistled, and it makes me feel kind of icky to analyze him. I'd just rather not think, or talk, about him, if that's okay."

"Of course that's okay," Cole said quickly. Smoothly, he flipped his hand over and intertwined his fingers with hers.

Oh shoot. Now they were holding hands again. She hadn't meant for that to happen. But she knew it would insult him if she suddenly ripped her hand away. Insult him, and probably hurt him. She didn't want to hurt him. In fact, she realized, she would do just about anything to *not* hurt him.

"Can I ask you a *different* personal question? Nothing to do with him, I think."

Oh boy. What did that mean? "You can ask, but I'm not sure I'll have an answer for you."

"Why *do* you hate music? I mean, I've never met anyone who claims to hate music altogether. There must be a reason."

She took a deep breath. Did she want to go there with him? Not really. But she was going to, wasn't she? Because what other choice did she have? "It's a long story."

"I've got time."

No, he didn't have time. Tomorrow he was going to leave town for a very long time. Maybe that would make this whole thing easier. She could open up to him, they could bond, and then he could ride off into the sunset, forget all about her, and she could get back to her regular life.

"It's my mom. Mary Jameson. She was a singer. I was born into this Music City nightmare, like a lot of kids were, I suppose, but my mom never got the rags to riches ending she planned on. My dad was a musician, I guess. That's what she said. I don't even know his name. Don't know if she did either. But she used to work the business really hard. She moved here as a teenager, had my brother super young. We don't know his father either. Anyway, she wrote songs, cut demos, even had a record with a small label that then promptly went out of business. Probably for cutting people like my mother. I don't know. She performed all over town whenever she could, *wherever* she could. She always said, 'You never know where you're going to get discovered,' which got silly when she was forty and everyone in town knew who she was and still no one wanted her. And she toured. A lot. I have memories of being in the van on the road for days on end. Darren and I would sit in cold parking lots while she was in the bar playing. And then she would come out drunk and either drive us to a motel or we would sleep right there in the parking lot." She paused to gulp for air. "And a few times, she never came out." She had *never* spilled it all out like this before. But the more she talked, the easier it got. "Sometimes we were cold. Sometimes we were hot. Often, we were hungry. Oh, she'd feed us if she could, but sometimes there just wasn't any money. Often she wouldn't get paid for gigs, even though she'd been promised she would be. She was terrible at the business side of it. Anyone else would have given up, but she didn't. She just kept fighting, kept believing in her stupid dream." She stopped talking and allowed herself to focus on an image of her mother on stage in a weak spotlight.

Cole squeezed her hand. "I'm so sorry. That sounds awful."

She tried to smile at him. "Yeah, it was. And she was always sorry too. She'd get drunk and go on and on about how much she loved us. And every morning, she'd apologize for the night before. The words quickly lost their meaning. *All* words lost meaning."

"She died?"

"Yeah. So, the older she got, the more I think she realized it just wasn't going to happen for her, and the more she drank. Eventually, she stopped touring, and Darren and I learned to fend for ourselves here. But she kept playing locally, and she kept right on partying. Back then, I was just a teenager, and I thought she was sort of the butt of the joke. Now, I'm not so sure if people were laughing at her. I mean, I was embarrassed of her, but she just was who she was, and I think people just thought she was a local artist who never got her break."

Cole shifted in his seat as if he was uncomfortable and turned his body toward her. "Makes me more grateful that I got my break."

"Well, you're crazy talented. And though I know some people are crazy talented and still don't get a break, I don't think she was."

"Was what?"

"Talented. I mean, she was solid. She could hit the right notes and she could play the guitar, but she didn't stand out. At least, that's how I saw it. That's what he was whistling, at first, one of her songs." She shook her head. She hadn't meant to let the conversation slip back to him.

She was grateful that Cole didn't let it keep going in that direction. "Well, thanks for calling me talented, but I think there was some providence involved with me. And probably with anyone who gets signed around here. So, how did she die?"

Lettie remembered the morning the police knocked on her door. "She had a gig at a dive bar called Sally's. It's gone now, been leveled and a new Starbucks is in its place. But she sang, and then she sat at the bar and drank. And drank. And drank. When they found her in her car, her blood alcohol content was 0.47. So I think she just passed out and never woke up. It was a relief, actually." She looked up at him sharply. "I know, that's a terrible thing to say."

He shook his head and looked into her eyes, and his eyes were so soft, so gracious. "You're just being honest."

"I was sixteen," she continued, unable to break his gaze. "I just wanted to be normal. I didn't want to worry about her anymore, to worry whether she was going to come home, to worry about her getting drunk and doing something embarrassing. She actually fell off a stage once. The ambulance came and everything. Anyway, I ..." Her voice faltered, and she stopped. *Don't cry, don't cry, don't cry.* But it was too late. The tears slid down her cheeks, and she tried to swat them away with the back of her hand, but they just kept coming.

"Go ahead, Lettie. Let it all out. It's okay to have feelings."

No, it wasn't. What good were feelings? Feelings were for songwriters, people who had time to moan about broken hearts. She was pragmatic. Life was what it was, and it wasn't good. You struggled to stay afloat and then you died. That was it. Nothing to cry about. But she didn't want to tell him any of that. Or she couldn't. So she just sat there crying and mortified that she was crying in front of him.

He slid closer and moved the hand he'd been holding to his other hand. Then he put his arm around her and pulled her close. Even though her brain told her this was a bad idea, her body nestled into him and she found she had her head on his chest, and it was so warm. She could hear his heart beating. It was the most beautiful music she'd ever heard.

23

Cole was a mess of conflicting emotions. He felt so much sympathy for Lettie. He was angry at her mother. He was angry at the music community for not sticking up for Darren and Lettie when they were young. He was sad for Mary, that her dreams never came true. He could imagine how crushingly disappointing that must have been for her. He felt helpless. There was nothing to be done about all this now, but he was desperate to fix it, to comfort Lettie, to make it all okay. And here he was holding Miss Goth in his arms, and it felt so right. But should it? She was not the wife he'd always dreamed of, the wife he'd *planned* on. Did she even want to have kids? He didn't want to fall in love with a woman who didn't want kids. And he couldn't believe he was even having these feelings. Why was he thinking about falling in love? He usually processed emotions by putting them into lyrics and melodies, but this story had at least twenty songs swimming around in it.

"So your name is Loretta. Who is Darren named after?"

Much to his delight, she laughed at this, and picked her head up a little. Her eyes were puffy and red. He guessed she didn't let herself grieve for her mother, or for the childhood she never had, very often. "Darren was a guitar player she toured with for a while. But he was good, and he got picked up for regular studio sessions, so she lost him. I mean, they were still friends, but he moved on to bigger and better things and left her behind. Everyone left her behind. Either they got more successful or they gave up and went home. But not my mom. She never gave up. Would have been so much easier if she had."

Cole searched his brain for words. He wanted to keep her talking. "I'm surprised you stayed in Nashville."

She shrugged. "It's my home. I got a job in high school, and I wanted to keep it. I needed the money. And all my friends were here—"

"You've been working at Maxwell's since high school?"

She smiled, sniffed, and shook her head.

He looked around the room for tissues, but didn't see any. He considered offering her his sleeve, but thought that might gross her out.

"No, no, not Maxwell's. I worked at a car wash. I loved that job, actually, but they got bought up by a chain and slashed everyone's hours and everyone's pay. I went to part-time for a while, but Maxwell's paid so much better, I just ended up going full-time there. It's really not so bad. They play music through the speakers, but no live garbage"—he flinched—"and I can usually control which station they play."

He shifted his weight around. His arm was falling asleep, but he didn't want to move. He was afraid she'd stop letting him hold her if he did. "I'm surprised a bar can even survive in this town without live music."

She looked contemplative. "Yeah, it's kept alive by locals who just want a place to drink without all the fuss. We have lots of regulars. Really nice people, most of them."

"That's cool." *Cool?* What a stupid thing to say. But he couldn't come up with anything better.

She sat up, and his stomach sank. "You've been so good to me." She wiped at her eyes. "Thank you. But I should probably get ready for my day, and I'm sure you've got stuff to do before you leave."

"Come with me." The words were out of his mouth before he had even realized he was going to say them.

The look on her face made him wish he could reach out, grab his words out of the air, and put them back into his mouth. "What?"

It was too late to back out now. "Lettie," he began, reaching out and taking her hand again. "I don't know what this is between us, exactly, but I think it's pretty obvious that there's something. And I know what I just said must seem a little weird ... or extreme maybe, but I don't want to leave you for months. I can find you a job on the tour." He had no idea if he could pull this off, but he'd worry about that after she said yes. "You'd get paid."

She snorted. "What kind of job could I have on a tour?"

"I don't know, but you're smart. I'm sure we could come up with something." He didn't want to use the word "roadie."

"You mean like a roadie?"

Well, there it was. "I don't know. Or personal assistant?"

She scowled. "Do you *need* a personal assistant?"

"Well, no, but I'm sort of shooting from the hip here. I just don't want to leave you."

She pulled her hand out of his and stood. "It's sweet of you to offer, but you're crazy. I'm not going on a country music tour, and no, I don't think that it's pretty obvious that there's anything going on between us. I rescued you from a bad situation. Now you've done the same. I'd say we're even." She folded her arms across her chest and looked at the ceiling without tipping her head up. It was almost as if she couldn't bear to look at him. "I'd say we could be friends, but that doesn't seem realistic either." She looked at him then. "You go on tour. You go be a big star. I'll be fine."

He stood up and tried to go to her, but she stepped back away from him. He didn't know what to do or say, so he just stood there like an idiot.

"You should go, Cole," she said softly. "But I really do appreciate your help. I won't need it again. Jason will be in jail for a while."

Jason? What did any of this have to do with Jason? Was that all he was to her? Someone to intervene when her stalker came around? He picked his hat up off her coffee table, put it on, tipped it to her, and then left her apartment. "Goodbye, Lettie," he said and then closed the door behind him.

24

Lettie watched him go and then sat back down on the couch and burst into tears. *I'm not even that sad. I'm just so tired.* She lay down and put her arm over her eyes. She had time for a nap before she went into work, and she was going to make good use of it. She couldn't believe he'd just tried to take her on tour with him. What did he think she was, a pet dog? She'd just finished telling him how much she hated the business, how she'd done enough "touring" for a lifetime, and then he had the gall to tell her to get on the bus? And then what? She'd work for him? Or she'd date him? What had he even meant by that invitation?

She rolled over and tried to get comfortable. These questions could go unanswered, because they didn't matter to her. They had nothing to do with her or with her life. Even if she could stand to date an artist, she did *not* want his white picket fence dream. She squeezed her eyes shut. She had to forget all about Cole Washburne. Somehow.

As tired as she was, sleep evaded her. She even got up and made herself a giant turkey sandwich and ate a whole bag of potato chips in an effort to sedate herself, but that only led to a stomachache—still no sleep. Finally, she gave up and got up off the couch. Then she stood in the shower, letting the hot water massage away her pain and confusion, until the water stopped being hot. She made herself some peppermint tea to try to offset her digestive discomfort and then headed for her car. Might as well go into work early. She needed to stay busy.

Max appeared happy to see her. "Ah, good, you're early. We need to talk."

Uh-oh. He *never* wanted to talk. To anyone. So this meant something. She didn't think she could take any more drama. She followed him to his tiny office that sat off the tiny kitchen. He sat down behind his cluttered desk, and she thought she was probably supposed to follow suit. She sat in an old, uncomfortable chair.

"You look tired."

He didn't know the half of it. "I had a rough night."

"I thought you didn't party."

"I don't." She took a deep breath. "There was some trouble in the neighborhood."

He looked intrigued by her statement, but she didn't want to expound on it.

"It's all over now. What's up?"

"Well, I've got some news." He leaned back in his chair and tried to pull one ankle up onto his knee. This looked like it hurt, but he pulled on the bottom of his pant leg until it happened. He was stalling. Whatever it was he had to tell her, he was worried she wasn't going to like it. Finally, he looked at her. "Someone's made an offer on this place."

What? What did that mean? "As in to *buy* it?"

"Yeah. And it's a good offer. I'm inclined to take it."

She tried to process the news, but it felt as though her brain was working in slow motion. Maybe that wasn't a bad thing. Slow processing was better than panic. "So are you telling me I'm out of a job?"

"Not necessarily, no. The new guy seems very pleasant and professional. He has said nothing to indicate to me that he wants to change my staff. Of course, I'll be leaving."

Of course. Why would she think otherwise?

"What I mean is, the place will change."

Of course it would change. What was he really trying to say?

"He's from away. Wants a piece of the Music City pie."

Oh. That's what he's dancing around. "He's bringing in performers?"

"Yeah. But not just singers," he hurried to say. "He says he wants comedians too. Even said something about a magician."

She could stand some humor in her life. Why didn't the new guy just open a comedy club? "So, I'm done here."

Max slowly shook his head. "You don't have to be, hon. That will be up to you."

Lettie nodded and use the armrests to push herself out of the chair. "Is that all?"

Max nodded, looking solemn. "Isn't that enough?"

She chuckled. "How long do we have?"

Max held up both hands. "This whole thing could fall through at any second. But if it goes through, we've got thirty days. You do a good job here, Lettie. The customers love you. I hope you'll stay on."

This news surprised her. She didn't think anyone loved her. And if they started having live music, would the bar even have the same customers? Wouldn't the music bring in a different kind of customer, driving the regulars elsewhere? So whether they loved her or not, she didn't know what she was going to do. No idea at all.

25

Cole stood in the heat of the stage lights at the Boston Garden in front of nearly twenty thousand fans. He'd never been to New England before. He'd never been to lots of places.

He was having the time of his life. Playing stadiums was everything he dreamed it would be. And this was only with a fifteen-minute set. He could only imagine how awesome it would be to headline, but for now, he was more than content. Life seemed perfect—except for the absence of Lettie, of course. She was always on his mind, even if she was just drifting around in the background. He missed her smirk. He missed her humor. He missed the smell of her hair, and the rush of adrenaline he felt whenever he was around her. But he tried not to dwell on what couldn't be and he ignored the urge to write a song about her, even though he had plenty of boring bus hours to do so. He knew she would hate it if he wrote about her, and so, even though she might never find out he had done so, he wasn't going to do it. He hadn't even finished his Lettie isn't funny song.

Despite the blinding lights, he could see the first few rows, and lots of people knew every word to his first single. It was the most gratifying feeling in the world, watching their lips move. He wanted to bring one of them up on stage with him to sing along, but that was not something an opening act could do. He would save that for when he was the bigwig. For now, he just tried to smile at them individually and connect with as many music lovers as possible. He and Branch weren't so different. His songs were a bit more raucous than the superstar's, but it wasn't much of a stretch to imagine Branch's fans becoming his fans.

He finished the song, stood there and enjoyed the fans' excitement and appreciation for the moment, and then gave them an enthusiastic goodbye wave and headed offstage. His turn was over. The Hammer Family was up next, who, despite their name making them sound like a heavy metal head-banging band, was a mother and her three kids playing bluegrass. They were so musically gifted, they made him feel like an impostor.

Out of the spotlight, he handed his guitar off to a stagehand and then stood to wait for the Hammers to take the stage.

Branch surprised him with a slap on the back. Cole looked up in surprise, and seeing who it was, tried to act cool. He didn't need to go all fan girl every time he encountered the man.

"Great job out there, man. You are really lighting it up. I might have to up my game, or they may be screaming at me to bring you back out on stage."

Cole laughed. "That's generous of you, Branch, but I don't see that happening."

Branch clicked his tongue. "I guess we'll have to see."

The crowd erupted as the Hammer Family walked out on stage.

"Of course, these guys are pretty amazing too. I've put quite the tour together, haven't I?"

Cole nodded, as Maggie Hammer began fingerpicking her mandolin. "These guys are crazy. How did you ever find them? I never heard of them until bam! they had a single on the radio."

"Would you believe I found them in a little church in Texas?"

Cole laughed, but he immediately thought of Lettie's mother. Some people worked their whole lives to make it and never did, and some people made it by accident. "Really? Were they looking to become professionals?"

"I don't think so, but I talked them into it. My cousin saw them play and told me about them, so I went to see for myself. Jumped out of the pew I was so excited." Branch laughed.

The youngest Hammer, Caleb, began to play his banjo. "How old is he?" Cole was incredulous.

"Twelve. Isn't he awesome? And then Elizabeth is fifteen, and Maggie is twenty-two. I'm not sure how old Mom is." He laughed. "I haven't asked."

"Smart move. Though she hardly looks older than her daughter. Maggie, I mean. She obviously looks older than Elizabeth." *Why am I an idiot?* He hated acting like a nervous schoolgirl around Branch. "But she doesn't look old," he added, in case anyone in earshot was going to report back to Serena Hammer that he'd said she looked old. He sucked in a lungful of air. "Is their name really Hammer?"

"Yeah, it sure is. What a stroke of luck, huh?" Branch slapped him on the back again. "Have a good night. I'm going to go to my bus and a down a couple of Cokes, see if I can get all sugared up for my show."

Cole laughed. He had stumbled onto the most sober tour in all of country music. That was fine by him. He didn't have time for alcohol. He had big plans—but for now, he was just going to relax and watch the Hammer Family do their thing, enjoy the fact that he was literally standing in one of his dreams, and try not to think about Lettie.

Their set was so good that it seemed to only last seconds. When it was over, he scooted to the side to let them leave the stage. As they did, Maggie Hammer sashayed by, flashing him a big smile that caught him off guard. As he stood there analyzing it, she returned and sidled up beside him. "You were awesome tonight. I am so impressed."

"Thank you. Much obliged."

She giggled. She was beautiful. Long, thick, wavy, dark blond hair, cute freckles across her nose, and a hypnotic smile. A pang of guilt stabbed at his chest, but he pushed it away. Lettie was out of reach. He had nothing to feel guilty about just noticing another woman's beauty. Besides, this one looked as though she *could* be wife material. At least, she didn't look like she'd just escaped from a tattoo parlor.

"I was wondering," she said coyly, "would you like to go get something to eat? We could go now ... or after the show?"

He looked at her, surprised. He wasn't used to being asked out by a girl. In fact, he didn't think it had ever happened before. "Uh ..."

She giggled again. "No pressure."

He definitely wanted to spend some time with this girl, didn't he? "Uh ... thanks for the offer, but I'm pretty beat."

Her face fell. "Oh, okay."

"Maybe some other time."

"Yeah, maybe." She turned and walked away.

"Good job out there," he called after her, but she kept walking. He didn't blame her.

26

Lettie delivered another pitcher of beer to table four and dodged what looked like it was going to be an unwelcome pat on her bottom. She liked serving, but it wasn't all fun and games. In recent years, she'd adored the boring life, because boring meant no drama from Jason, but with him safely tucked away, maybe she could shake things up a bit. Was it time for a change? But what? What else could she do? She was pretty smart, sure, but she had no skills that she knew of. She couldn't fix anything, wasn't artistic, wasn't good with computers. She cleared a table, sighing in resignation that maybe she *was* destined to serve beer for the rest of her life. Things could be worse.

Wait. She *did* have another option, didn't she? Cole had offered her a job.

She was surprised at how much the idea didn't horrify her. She could be a roadie. Roadies didn't necessarily have to listen to the music, did they? She held up a finger to Stan, a thirsty regular, who was beckoning her as she headed toward a table of newcomers. She could ask Cole specifically for a job that would keep her as far from the music as possible. That would be okay, right? "Hi, I'm Lettie. What can I get you?" She nodded as they made their requests, but her head was spinning. Oh, how she missed Cole, but what she was considering was mad. Go out on the road with a bunch of country music artists? She laughed aloud at herself as she headed for the bar.

Max raised his eyebrows at her. "You okay?"

She shrugged. She had no idea if she was okay. There was a good chance she was losing her mind. "One pale ale, one Bud, and a hurricane, please."

"Coming right up."

"And I think Stan wants another."

Max nodded, flipped the tap on and off, and then set a foaming mug on the bar. Lettie grabbed it and headed Stan's way.

"Have a seat. Take a load off," Stan said as he pushed his empty mug toward the edge of the table.

"Where's Phil?" Stan's usual drinking pal was missing.

"I don't know. He'll be around shortly, I suspect. Here"—he patted the table—"join me."

"Can't, Stan. I've got work to do."

He swore in disbelief. "It's not even busy. And something's obviously bothering you. Max won't care if you keep me company for a minute."

She didn't want to sit, but her tip would be improved by it, as long as other tippers didn't get disgusted that she was resting while they were in need. She slid into the booth. "Nothing is bothering me."

He swore again. "You can't lie to an old dog."

She didn't think this was a saying, but she wasn't sure. "No, really."

"Tell Stan all about it."

She took a deep breath. Was she really tempted to ask Stan for advice? This was ridiculous.

"Come on. I've been around the barn a time or two."

She didn't think this was a saying either. "I'm just ... well, you know how this place is going to change ownership, right?"

He nodded, obviously expecting more.

"Well, I'm just wondering if I should stick around."

He still expected more.

"Or not," she added.

He nodded again. "Well, Lettie, it's been my experience that sometimes you've just got to plug your nose and jump right into the deep end."

What? Well, you get what you pay for, and advice from drunk people is free. "Okay." She didn't know what else to say.

"Yeah, it is okay. That's what I'm trying to tell you, if you'd just listen. You're thinking about jumping, which means you want to jump. And I don't mean off a building or anything. I mean into a new life. So if you want to jump, then jump! Don't just keep thinking about it, because then you'll never do it. You just got to jump."

That actually made a bizarre sort of sense. "Okay then. Thanks, Stan."

"You bet. Anytime, Lettie. Anytime."

She gave him a small smile that she hoped conveyed gratitude and then went back to the bar. She still had a few weeks to decide. But what if Cole recanted on his offer? She should call him and make sure the offer still stood, but Max would be super annoyed if he caught her on the phone again. So she'd wait and call Cole later. Or maybe she should text him—that would be less invasive. She'd also check his tour schedule. She didn't even know where he was. The idea of seeing him again made her giddy, and this feeling frustrated her. She was going to take a job from him—nothing else. Sure, he was wonderful and all that, but just *no*. That was a deep end she was afraid she'd drown in.

27

Cole didn't want to go out with Maggie Hammer, did he? Had he made a mistake? Shoot. He'd definitely made a mistake. He pulled his hat down and chased after her.

"Maggie! Maggie!" He trotted down the hallway feeling like a fool. Finally, he caught sight of her just before she ducked into her dressing room. "Maggie! Wait up!"

She spun around to face him.

"You know what? We've got a long drive tonight, and I can sleep in tomorrow. So sure, let's go find some food."

"Great!" she said, sounding far perkier than Lettie ever had. Wait, why was he comparing her to Lettie? That wasn't fair to either of them. "Just let me change. I'll be right out." She flashed him a perfect smile full of perfect teeth and then turned and went into the dressing room.

He stood there, feeling like some sort of a peeping tom hanging around outside the women's dressing room. But she soon reappeared in a jean jacket, tight jeans he tried not to look too closely at, and a pair of really high heels. *I guess she's not planning on walking anywhere.* Oh shoot. Where *were* they going? He didn't know anything about Boston, let alone their immediate surroundings. "Uh ..." he tried.

She grabbed his arm and leaned into him. "Are you trying to give me a compliment?"

No, he wasn't, but he probably should. "Yes, you look lovely." *And you must really love denim.* "Also, do you have a plan for where we're going?" He felt like a chump.

"Not really." She started walking. She walked like she had a plan. He tagged along. "But we could just grab a cab."

Right. Why hadn't he thought of that?

They stepped outside, and the city seemed alive around them. Noise, lights, and scents surrounded him, and he felt like an overwhelmed hick who'd just come down out of the hills. Nashville was a city—a huge city, but it had somehow always felt *doable.* He wasn't so sure about this city.

She took her phone out of her small purse.

"Calling a cab?"

"Uber."

"What?"

"I'm getting us an Uber. I just thought it would be easier."

"Oh."

After a few swipes across the screen, she held it up to him. "See? That little car is our guy. He'll be here in just a few minutes."

"Great. And then where are we going?"

"How about Mac's Burgers? It's like two minutes away."

Two minutes? Maybe they could walk. Then he remembered her shoes and the fact that this city was complicated. He looked around. Even getting out of the parking lot looked tricky.

"You were so good tonight," she said, leaning into him.

He smiled at her. "You too. Your family is so talented. How long have you been playing?"

"Playing what?" She giggled.

He didn't get the joke. "The mandolin."

"Oh. I don't know, five years, maybe? But I also play the piano and the drums."

He raised his eyebrows. "A drummer, huh?"

"Yeah, but my mother won't let me play drums for us." Resentment was woven through her words.

"That makes sense. Not a lot of bluegrass bands with drummers."

"Bluegrass," she repeated as if the word tasted bad in her mouth.

He didn't know what to say to that, so he tried to look up at the stars, but there weren't any. They stood in companionable silence for a few minutes, her still holding onto his arm, but then she tugged on it. "He's here."

"Okay." He followed her to the car, and they climbed in.

"Hi!" she said brightly. "Can you take us to Mac's Burgers? It's at 2112 Bowkery Way."

"Sure thing. You guys roadies?"

She giggled. "No, we're the opening acts."

"Oh, cool. Can I have your autographs? You might be famous one day."

"Sure." Maggie took a notepad out of her purse. "What's your name?"

"Tobias."

She scribbled something onto the paper, ripped it out, handed it up front to Tobias, who didn't look at it, and then slid the pad back into her purse. Cole wasn't crushed. Signing an autograph for Tobias hadn't been a lifelong dream, but he still felt a little slighted. *She just forgot about me,* he told himself, but part of him knew this wasn't true.

"Here we go!" Tobias said, pulling up in front of a neon burger joint.

"Thanks, Tobias," Maggie said, already opening the door. "I tipped you through the app."

"You bet!"

Cole climbed out of the car, and before he'd even stood up straight, Maggie had hold of his arm again. They went into the blessedly empty restaurant; he removed his hat and watched Maggie slide into the closest booth, facing the door. Cole wanted to argue, but he didn't. He always sat facing the door, especially when he was with a woman. It made him feel safer, like he could protect her better from that vantage point, though, he was willing to admit, if some crazed gunman came into the burger joint, it probably wouldn't matter which side of the table he was sitting on. He sat down on the other side of the table.

A server was there in seconds and slapped two dirty, plastic menus down in front of them. "Do you know what you want to drink?" she asked, through a mouthful of gum and a thick accent. Her name tag read Rochelle.

"Can I get an orange pop, please?"

"Diet Coke," Maggie said, without looking up from her phone.

Wordlessly, Rochelle vanished, and Cole, feeling resolutely ignored, opened his menu. He wasn't even hungry. Why had he come on this adventure again? Oh yeah, Maggie was pretty.

He found something that sounded palatable and then closed his menu. Maggie was still playing with her phone.

She did put it down when Rochelle reappeared with drinks.

"Is this on one check?" she asked, taking a small pad out of her apron.

"Yes," Maggie said before he could open his mouth to answer. She finally flipped the menu open and then scanned its pages with a distasteful look on her face. "What's a Cape Cod Salad?" she asked without looking at Rochelle.

"It's got arugula, bacon, blue cheese—"

"Sounds good," Maggie said, though it was clear Rochelle wasn't done with her definition.

Cole was embarrassed and decided then to leave a big tip. "Could I please have the chili burger?" He smiled and handed her his menu.

Maggie didn't offer hers, but Rochelle took it anyway.

Maggie crossed her hands in front of her and smiled at him. Apparently, she was going to pay attention to him now. "So, what's it like growing up in South Dakota?"

He shrugged. He wasn't in the mood for bonding, but he didn't want to be rude. "I'm from Wyoming. And I don't know. Country is country, I guess. Lots of fields and dirt roads."

She smiled, as her eyes flicked to the door behind him, and then back to him. Was she expecting someone? "And did you grow up on a farm?" Her eyes flicked again. It was almost as if she wasn't aware of what her own eyes were doing.

"A ranch, yeah. Small one. My dad raises cattle."

"Oh, wow, neat."

He was confident she had no idea what he'd just said. "So what about you? You're from Texas?"

"Yep. Born and raised. But my mom was a third grade teacher, and my dad is a bus driver. Not exactly the makings of a hit song."

"Your dad still is a bus driver?"

"Yeah, except he traded in the big yellow bus for the tour bus." She curled her upper lip. It would have been cute if she wasn't being so negative.

"Oh my gosh!" someone chirped from behind him. Then she squealed as she appeared to his right. "Hi!" The young woman stuck out her hand to Maggie. "I'm Abby! This is my friend, Chan."

Chan stood silently beside Abby, clearly less excited than she was about whatever was happening.

Abby turned to Cole. "Hi, I'm Abby," she said again. "I *love* your new song!"

"Thanks." He was bewildered.

"Can I have your autograph?" Abby asked, but it was unclear whom she was speaking to—maybe both of them?

"Sure!" Maggie said.

Abby had nothing to autograph. "Oh, wait." She reached for a napkin out of the napkin holder on their table. In her exuberance, she would've knocked Cole's pop into his lap if he hadn't grabbed it. Chan gave him an apologetic look.

Like magic, Maggie had a Sharpie in her hand, and signed the napkin. Then she slid it across the table to Cole, who didn't know what else he could do but follow her lead.

"Want to take a selfie with us?" Maggie asked, her voice far too high-pitched to sound authentic.

"Yeah!" Abby's enthusiasm was definitely authentic.

"Great." Maggie stood up, scooted in front of them, and then slid in beside Cole. "Give me your phone and stand behind us."

Wowsa, she was bossy.

Abby and Chan followed instructions, and Maggie held the phone up in front of them. Then, just before she snapped the shot, she leaned over and kissed Cole on the cheek. He jumped and then felt bad. Surely that was some sort of insult, but he hadn't been expecting to feel her lips on his cheek. He had liked the feel of them, and yet felt a little violated.

"Do you have Twitter?" Maggie said, handing the phone back.

Abby nodded. "Of course!"

Chan rolled his eyes.

"Great! Be sure to tag me when you post the picture, and then I'll retweet for you! Thanks for stopping by!" She stood up, folded her fingers at them in something resembling a wave, and then sat back down, effectively dismissing them.

Cole waited for them to leave, waited for the air to settle, and then asked, "How did they know you were here?"

She took a sip of her pop and batted her eyelashes at him. "I posted it."

"Posted it where?"

She gave him a small smile. "Everywhere."

His phone buzzed. He looked down at it and was beyond thrilled to see Lettie's name on the screen. Oh, thank God. He *was* going to get to talk to her again. But not right now. He didn't want to be rude to Maggie, no matter how obnoxious she was being.

"Who is that?"

"A friend. I'll call her back later. So, do you have more fans coming?"

"I hope so. But we are not exactly in country country, and I'm not famous—yet."

He suddenly needed a break. "I'll be right back. I'm going to use the restroom." He took his time getting to the bathroom and washing his hands once he got there. This had better be one heck of a burger.

He grudgingly left the safety of the solitude. When he stepped out of the bathroom, Maggie had his phone in her hands. He quickened his pace. "What's going on?"

She quickly put the phone down. "I was just seeing if you had Twitter on your phone."

"Oh." He wasn't sure if she was telling the truth. "I don't."

"I saw that."

28

Lettie forced herself to put her phone on the nightstand. He wasn't going to respond. He hadn't answered her call, which she understood, but now he wasn't answering her text either. She tried not to be hurt. She knew he was busy. She'd checked his schedule, and they had a show in Boston that night. She wondered what it would be like to go to Boston. She'd never been north of Virginia. She never would have been anywhere other than Tennessee if not for her mother's own tour dates. She took a deep breath. What was she doing? After all she'd been through, was she really going to go back out *on tour* with someone? In a way, the idea sounded absurd. In a way, it scared her. In a way, it felt like slipping into a pair of comfy jeans. Yes, she thought she *was* going to go.

Even if she didn't get fired, she was still effectively losing her job. And she missed Cole so much. Even if they were never together, she still wanted to be around him. So yes, she was going to go, as crazy as that was. But first, he had to text her back. Or all bets were off.

She rolled onto her side, away from the nightstand, and pulled the covers up over her head. She squeezed her eyes shut and tried not to think about anything, tried to let herself drift into slumber.

Just when she thought she wasn't going to succeed in falling asleep, she did. And she dreamed about Cole. He was riding a horse over a rocky trail, looking like something out of a 1960s western, not that she'd seen a lot of those, but that was the association her brain made. He looked so tall and proud in the saddle. He looked ... well ... gorgeous. In the dream, she tried to stop looking at him, but he rode right up to her and dismounted with grace. Then he tipped his hat to her. "Howdy, Miss." She laughed at him. She tried to make fun of him, but in the dream, she couldn't talk. Well, that was annoying. Then the scene changed, and he was lying beside a small campfire with his bedroll under his neck and his hat over his face. Again, just like the old westerns. Wondering if there would soon be a gunfight, she lay down beside him and rested her head on his chest. Another scene shift. Now he was waist-deep in a small, calm pool of water. Oh dear! She tried to look away. She shouldn't be watching him swim, or bathe, or whatever he was doing. But she couldn't move her eyes. He smiled at her, and then, in an instant, he turned into a bald eagle and flew away.

She sat bolt upright in bed, wide awake. She knew she'd dreamed about Cole, and she felt guilty for some reason, but the dream was already fading, and she couldn't remember what she'd done in the dream to feel guilty about. She figured maybe she was better off not knowing.

She lay back down, accepting that sleep might not visit again soon, and picked up her phone. Still no answer from Cole. *Maybe I should see how the tour's going.* She knew Cole didn't tweet, but she thought maybe Branch did. She found Branch's profile, but he hadn't tweeted in months. *I guess stars that big don't have to tweet.* There was someone else on the tour, though, right? She spent a few minutes with Google and figured out that the Hammer Family was along for the ride. She soon found their official Twitter account, which was silent, but the family's bio linked her to their individual accounts. And that's how she ended up with a sick feeling in her stomach, staring at Maggie Hammer's most recent retweet, which she'd captioned, "Having a burger with @ColeWashburne and some friends."

There he was, with Miss Hammer's lips on his cheek. He had the strangest expression on his face, as if he hadn't expected the picture to be taken, as if he was being caught in the act of something. Of course, this was absurd. He wasn't being caught at anything. He was single. He could be kissed by as many women as he wanted. At least this one wasn't married. At least, Lettie didn't think so.

It looked like they were sitting in a diner, with two people Lettie didn't recognize in the background. So that's why he hadn't answered her call. He was out with other people. And of course he was. What did she think was going to happen when he went off on tour, that he was going to stay on the bus pining away after her? No, it made sense that he was out on the town with people. It made sense he was with Maggie Hammer. They were touring together, they had lots in common, and she was beautiful. Lettie wondered if they were officially dating. It seemed awfully soon, but maybe he'd already known her, before he went on tour with her?

Yes, she decided. They were probably dating. And if they weren't, they would be. And that was okay. Because no matter what weird feelings she was having for the man, she and he could never be together. So it was good that he was getting to know someone else, someone who *made sense* for him. Someone who could love and appreciate his music and give him the white picket fence he'd always wanted—the whole kit and caboodle.

She returned the phone to the nightstand and tried to fall back asleep. But it was a long time coming.

THE NEXT MORNING, HER phone rang, and Cole's name appeared on her screen. She ignored his call.

He texted her a few minutes later. "Sorry I missed your call. What's up?"

She didn't answer him.

She wasn't going to go on tour with him. That had been a silly idea. She would just deal with whatever Maxwell's was going to be. And if that didn't work out, she could be a waitress anywhere. Maybe it was even time to leave Nashville.

After her shower, she deleted all of his contact info from her phone. She didn't want to be tempted to change her mind.

29

On stage for sound check, Cole could feel Maggie staring at him. Her eyes reminded him of a barn cat's, laser-focused on him with an occasional darting to the corners of the room to look out for predators. He'd never seen a woman as jumpy as Maggie Hammer.

He finished his song, waited for the all-clear from the sound guys, and then tried to exit the stage while giving himself as wide a berth as possible from Miss Hammer.

It didn't matter. She was at the bottom of the steps before he got there. "You sounded so awesome, Cole!"

He smiled, genuinely enjoying the praise. She might be a little crazy, but she was also crazy-talented and beautiful, and he enjoyed her admiration. "Thank you." He tipped his hat to her and tried to walk by.

She stepped to the side to block his way. "Aren't you going to hang out for my sound check?"

My not *our*. He felt bad for Maggie's mother. "You mean *your family's* sound check?"

She put a hand on one hip and rolled her eyes. "Whatever. My family's just riding my coattails. You know that I'm the one everyone comes to see."

He knew no such thing. "Uh ... actually, I'd like some downtime before the show. I'm sure you can understand." He tried to muster up a friendly smile.

She frowned. "Actually, I don't understand. You've done nothing since last night's show."

Oh, so now she's keeping tabs on me?

"What could you possibly need to recover from?" She folded her arms across her chest.

His brain scrambled for a way to remain polite but also extricate himself from the situation.

His brain came up with nothing.

Maggie's mother called her up on stage, and Maggie gave her a look that could have fried an egg. Then she returned her eyes to Cole, and they immediately softened.

If he wasn't so certain that she didn't like him, he might be fooled into thinking she did. "You'd better get up there," he said and brushed by her toward the exit. He knew he'd probably made her mad, but after last night's shenanigans, he cared less about angering her. He had no interest in being ensnared in whatever social media publicity scheme she was cooking up. On his way back to his bus, he checked his phone, for the zillionth time that day, to see if Lettie had answered him.

But she hadn't. That was so weird. She was the one who had called him, and now she wouldn't call or text again? Maybe she *had* texted, and maybe Maggie had deleted it when she was fiddling with his phone. Nah, Maggie wouldn't go that far. Maybe Lettie was just busy. But, doing what? She didn't work in the mornings. As far as he knew, she didn't do anything in the mornings. Except, apparently, ignore him. Oh well. He needed to move on with his life anyway, start fresh, find a nice, normal girl he could settle down with. Enough with all the drama.

"Hey, Cole!" Shawn called from behind.

Cole turned to face him.

Shawn caught up to him, sounding a little out of breath. "Hey, we got a radio interview for you tomorrow morning. Six o'clock sharp."

Awesome. Cole loved those spots. They were like old school country music touring, connecting with the people in the most tried-and-true way, while they were doing morning chores or while they drove to work. "Great. Thanks."

"You're welcome. Now, have you been on Twitter today?"

Cole snorted.

Shawn smiled. "I didn't think so. Maggie Hammer has managed to kick up a small dust storm. It's no big deal, but I got one call asking if you two were an item. I told them no ... but I'm not wrong, am I?"

Something in Shawn's voice made Cole feel defensive of Maggie. "Would that be such a bad thing?"

Shawn shook his head quickly. "No, no, of course not. It might even be a good thing, publicly, but ... privately, I'm not so sure." He looked pensive, as if he was reconsidering what he'd just said. "Actually, I'm not even sure it would be good publicly. Right this second, it would be great for your image, but I've got a feeling she's a bit of a loose cannon, so if your image gets caught up with her image, and then she goes off the deep end—"

Cole snickered. "I don't think she's going to go off the *deep end*, Shawn."

"Maybe not, but I've seen her type before. She might be a bit too tightly wound for this life."

Cole didn't know what he meant, and his face must have betrayed his cluelessness.

"I don't mean to insult her," Shawn said quickly. "She's young, and she may adjust. But right now, she's just a little ..." It seemed he was searching for words. "I don't know. So, are you an item or not?"

"Definitely not." The speed with which the words flew out of his mouth surprised Cole.

Shawn slapped him on the shoulder. "Good then. Go ahead and let her post her selfies with you. I'll tell everyone you guys are just good friends. Bonding on the road and all that. Fans love that stuff."

Cole nodded. "If you say so."

"Trust me. This is what I do." He gave Cole a smile that was probably meant to be reassuring and then turned toward the arena.

"Thanks, Shawn."

Shawn waved over his head, without turning around. "It's what you pay me for," he called back.

Cole took out his phone, scrolled through his contacts, and pressed Lettie's name. Maybe she hadn't seen that he'd called last time. Maybe she hadn't seen his text. Maybe she'd lost her phone. Maybe she hadn't paid her bill and her phone had been turned off and as soon as she paid the bill, she'd call him. He ended the call before it began. Shoot. He hated feeling so silly. He didn't need to pester the woman. If she wanted to talk to him, she'd call.

He couldn't believe how much he wanted to talk to her. He wanted to tell her about Maggie and hear her make fun of the whole charade. Maggie was all plastic, designer clothes; thick, perfect makeup; and cloying perfume. She looked fabulous, but the sum of her made him miss Lettie, who was *real*. She was who she was, for better or for worse, and he missed that person. In fact, in that moment, he wished he missed her a little less.

30

Lettie was relieved to hear Max call out, "Last call" and annoyed to see a man she didn't recognize walk in immediately afterward. The timing was so perfect she thought it might have been purposeful, though who on earth waits outside a bar until the bartender announces imminent closing? He came in, quickly casting his eyes around the place, and sat down at an empty table in the corner. How bizarre. It would make more sense if he'd already been drinking that evening, but he looked sober as a switchblade.

Though she didn't want to, she approached him, mustering up the best it's-almost-closing-time smile she could.

He watched her coming.

She was certain she'd never seen him before, yet there was something hauntingly familiar about his eyes. "I'm sorry, but Max already gave last call. We'll be closing soon." Once she got close enough, she could see how haggard he looked. His skin was leathery and wrinkled, and his eyelids were so droopy he looked sleepy. His haircut was at least thirty years out of date, but he tried to make up for it with copious amounts of gel.

"Loretta," he said in a gravelly voice.

She started. No one ever called her that. Most people didn't even know it was her name. Who *was* this guy? "Do I know you?"

He shrugged. "You don't, and I'm sorry for that." He shifted in his chair, and it creaked. At least, she thought it was the chair creaking. It could have been his bones. "My name is Ronnie." He paused, and a sense of dread filled her. Even though her brain had no idea what he was about to say, some part of her did. That's the only thing that could explain that dread. "I'm your father, honey."

She swore. "No, you're not." She stared at him, trying to glean something—anything—from the sight of him, but there were no answers there. Only a stranger's face. "Please," she said, her voice thick but quiet, "show yourself out." She turned to walk back to the bar. She wasn't a drinker, but she was thinking about pouring herself a shot or two.

"Mary told me I was the father."

At the sound of her mother's name on this man's lips, her eyes burned with tears. She stopped walking but didn't turn around. What was there to say? Who knew what was true? If this guy was her biological father, so what? It didn't mean anything.

She started walking again, opened the bar flap, slipped behind it, and then lowered it shut, breathing a sigh of relief at the barrier—however flimsy—it provided. Her sense of relief didn't last because he soon approached her. "Look, I'm not trying to make trouble. I just want to be a part of your life."

Oh, she was so *not* going to do this. "I'm sorry you wasted your time, but I'm just not interested." She tried to get Max's attention with her eyes, but he was busy flirting with one of his favorite customers. Lettie didn't know what, exactly, she wanted Max to do, but she thought maybe he'd do *something*.

But this guy wasn't going to go away easily. "Look, I just want to talk to you." His voice now had an edge to it. He must have noticed, because it immediately softened. "I just want to get to know you, to be part of your life."

Since when? Sure, she had questions she wanted to ask him: Why now? How long had he known he'd had a daughter? Why had he abandoned her? Why had he never tried to get in touch before tonight? But she wasn't going to ask any of those questions, because she wasn't going to engage with the man. At all.

A sudden thought felt like a knife to her gut. Maybe he needed something. A kidney? Part of her liver? Bone marrow? Oh yeah, that would be rich. She glared at him and tried to be as persuasive as possible, as she said, slowly, taking great care to enunciate, "I don't want you to be part of my life. Now go."

He blinked. She didn't know him from Adam, but she could tell he hadn't liked that. He put his hands on the bar and leaned toward her, his eyes narrowed. She stepped back reflexively. Finally, she saw Max look over at them and head their way. The man who called himself Ronnie whispered, "You're my daughter, and if you're hooking up with a big star, I'm getting my piece of the pie."

She barked out a laugh. She was disgusted, but mostly she was relieved. Was that all? "I'm not hooking up with any star, so you can go back to your life."

"Everything okay here?" Max said, keeping his hand below the bar. There was nothing in that particular spot to grab, but he always did that so that people would wonder what was down there. Ten feet farther down the bar there was a baseball bat. Lettie had heard that Max had only had to use it once—before her time.

"Everything's peachy," Ronnie said without taking his eyes off Lettie. "This is none of your concern."

"I'm making it my concern. And we're closing, so, can you find the door, or do you need some help?"

Ronnie looked at Max, looked him up and down, resting his eyes for a moment on the bar above the hand he couldn't see. Then he stood up straight. Oh thank goodness, he was leaving. He took a step backward, and Max stepped closer to Lettie, a gesture of protectiveness that would have annoyed her under other circumstances.

Then Ronnie stopped moving. "Don't lie to me, you little hussy. I'm a fan of the up-and-coming Cole Washburne, and I think I might just go pay him a visit." When he said "up-and-coming," his voice was thick with sarcasm. He swallowed as he took another step back, and then he hissed, "He should know your family, after all." And then he was gone.

Lettie exhaled and looked at Max. Only then did she realize everyone else in the bar was staring at her. Her cheeks got hot. Oh, fantastic. Now *she* was the show. "What the heck was that?" she asked Max, as if he knew.

"You okay?"

She didn't know the answer to that. "I'm fine. But I don't know what he just meant. He's going to 'go see' Cole? How? The guy's on tour? And we're not even together. He won't be able to get close to him."

Max walked away with a shrug. "I dunno. I wouldn't worry about it." He was already done worrying. He was done with the situation altogether. He wanted to close up and go home, just like every other night.

"It almost sounded like a threat," she said, sort of to Max, but mostly just to herself. Would that weird man try to harm Cole? Would he hurt him physically? Embarrass him? Interfere with his career? Lettie felt sick to her stomach. Maybe she should have asked the guy for clarification.

She couldn't get out of the bar fast enough. Max didn't say anything, but it seemed he understood her frenzy. She had made it halfway to her car out back when she changed her mind and headed back inside.

Max looked up. "Forget something?"

She stopped. How should she phrase the question when she didn't even know what she was asking? Her mouth hung open.

"If you need a day off," Max said, somehow understanding her situation better than she did, "just call in the morning."

"But—"

"We'll manage without you. I don't *want* to, but we will. You take care of what you need to do." He gave her a solemn nod that said his word was firm and she should go home.

"Okay. Thanks, Max. You're the best."

"Don't I know it," he said and flicked off the Christmas lights that circled the mirror behind the bar year-round.

Grateful for his understanding, she headed back for her car, her brain agonizing over her options. She had to warn Cole, didn't she? But how? She'd deleted his contact info. It would be easy to find him, but she'd have to travel. But would this Ronnie guy seriously go to the trouble to travel to Cole, or was he just making idle threats? Were they even really threats? Was she making a mountain out of a mole hill? Jason had trained her to think all men were crazy. Maybe Ronnie wasn't crazy enough to stalk a country music star.

She couldn't even search for Ronnie online. She didn't know his last name. Her brother could find the scoop, she knew he could, but she didn't want to involve Darren. She wanted to figure this out for herself.

She groaned as she settled into the driver's seat. She locked the door behind her, leaned back on the headrest, and closed her eyes. Maybe she should just do nothing. Cole was a big boy; he could take care of himself. But didn't she owe him a warning if there was a threat? Or was she just using this as an excuse to see him? If she was honest with herself, she had to admit she *really* wanted to see him, whether or not he was involved with that Hammer chick.

The Hammer chick! Of course! Why hadn't she thought of that? Cole didn't do Twitter, but Maggie Hammer certainly did. Lettie opened her Twitter app and then thought. She couldn't private message Maggie, because Maggie didn't follow her. That meant she had to send a public tweet. But she didn't want the whole world to know that she might have a father who might be crazy and might be after Cole Washburne. So she tweeted: @RealMagsHammer, This is Cole's friend. Please tell him to call Lettie. IMPORTANT!

There. That should work. If Maggie would pass it on. Lettie wasn't sure that she would. If they were dating, Maggie might be feeling a bit possessive of Cole. This thought made *her* feel a smidge possessive. Lettie really missed him. She checked her app, even though it had only been thirty seconds. No response. She went to Maggie's profile to make sure her tweet had been sent, and couldn't believe what she saw. Maggie had blocked her. Oh *wow*, the chick was nuts. Lettie was surrounded by nutty people. She thought it was safe to assume Maggie wasn't going to deliver the message.

She tried to ignore her annoyance about that and make a practical decision. Plan B. She could try contacting any of them through Facebook, but she didn't think Cole would see such a thing, and she thought Maggie would probably just block her again.

She checked Cole's schedule and impatiently jiggled her leg up and down, shaking the whole car, as the web page loaded. Finally, the tiny screen told her that he would be in Moline the following evening. *Moline?* She'd never even heard of it. She opened her map app. Good grief, it was an eight-hour drive. She kicked herself for deleting his contact info. This would be so much easier if she could just call him.

She started her car and put it in drive. She would sleep on it and decide in the morning.

Except she couldn't sleep. She tossed and turned, wrestling with the variables. *If* Ronnie was just full of hot air, then she would go to Moline for nothing, and Cole would think she was zany. But Cole was too kind to think that. He would be sweet about the whole thing; she knew he would. And *if* Ronnie really was a threat, well, then, didn't she *have* to warn Cole? Wasn't it zany not to?

She had to go. She would go. Everyone should go to Moline, Illinois at least once in their life. She would pack a bag, leave a note for her roommate, and hit the road first thing in the morning. As she planned what she would write in that note, she finally drifted off to sleep.

31

Moline, Illinois. Cole was excited to be in yet another new city, especially to be in the home of John Deere. The venue in Moline was on the smallish side, so their first show had sold out months ago, and Branch had booked a second show. That meant two nights in a row in the same city, which meant a hotel room for the night. Cole really didn't mind sleeping on the bus. He found it exciting and enjoyed the hum of the road underneath him. But he was also looking forward to sleeping in an actual bed.

The bus pulled into the parking lot of the hotel, and Cole was still stretching, trying to get his land legs under him, when he looked up to see Maggie coming down the narrow aisle.

"Good morning!" she said, all bright-eyed and bushy-tailed. She was already dressed to kill, with bright pink shiny lips and some fuzzy white thing around her neck.

"Morning." He did not match her enthusiasm.

"What are your plans for the day?"

He didn't really have any. Not yet, anyway. "Just going to relax in the hotel, I guess. Watch some TV. Maybe check out the pool."

"Oh yeah! The pool will be great! But let's go out first."

"Go out? It's ten o'clock in the morning."

"We could get brunch!"

He sighed. He didn't know what to do with this girl. "Maybe," he said, because he didn't know what else to say. Then he looked at the door of the bus. "Let's go check in, and then we'll see what happens."

There was a long line at the front desk, which gave Maggie ample time to chat his ear off about last night's show and a nearby zoo. He zoned out for most of it, but then he realized she was staring at him, waiting for him to answer some question he hadn't heard. "I'm sorry, what?"

"I asked if you wanted to be in my video."

Her video? "You mean a Hammer Family video?"

She rolled her eyes. "I don't know. Maybe we'll do it, but if not, I'll just do it myself. Weren't you listening?"

He nodded. "Of course."

"Right." She didn't believe him. "I don't think my mom would be into the theme I'm thinking of." She held up both her hands like claws and made a loud meow sound that embarrassed him in the crowded lobby. "I said that I wanted to put on tiger stripes and cool makeup, and like, show my wild side."

Cole couldn't imagine which Hammer Family song would match that theme. "Okay," he said, his doubt audible.

"Fine. Don't get excited. When I make it happen, I'll re-invite you. You can be my tiger's prey." She held her claws up again, but this time, he was grateful, she didn't meow.

Finally, someone handed him his room key, and he headed for the elevator. She was right behind him. He hoped she was on a different floor. He was starting to feel a bit smothered. "What room do you have?" he asked without thinking, and then cringed at how that sounded.

Her face lit up. "Five fifteen."

Oh good. He was on the fourth floor. He smiled at her. "Cool. Maybe I'll give you a call after I settle in. But if you don't want to wait for me, you go right ahead. I don't think I want to go to the zoo." If he was going to do anything, he'd tour the John Deere factory, but he didn't even think he wanted to do that. He really wanted to lounge around and enjoy the hotel, watch television or sit in the hot tub.

When he realized she'd followed him off the elevator onto the fourth floor, he stopped walking and turned to face her. "This isn't your floor."

"I know," she said perkily. "I wanted to see your room."

Oh good grief. This had to stop. He took a deep breath. "Maggie, I don't mean to hurt your feelings, but I'm not interested in anything other than friendship with you."

She recoiled as if he'd slapped her. "Excuse me?"

His stomach rolled with guilt. "I mean no offense. You're beautiful and talented and ... I am just not interested in a relationship right now." That was probably the biggest lie he'd ever told.

"Relationship?" she screeched. "Who said anything about relationship? I'm just trying to have a little fun."

"Right." His brain searched for words. "I just don't work like that. If I'm going to date someone, it's going to be with an eye to the future."

"The future?" She sneered. "You just said you don't want a relationship, but you're thinking about the future?"

He was sunk. "I don't know how to explain it, Maggie, but I want to be clear with you that I'm not interested in anything with you other than a professional relationship."

Her jaw dropped, and he could hardly stand to look at her. How had this gotten so awkward? He wasn't usually such a bumbling idiot. "Oh, is that how it is? Fine!" She took a step closer to him. "I didn't like you, anyway. You're nothing special. I just thought you could help my career." And then she spun on her incredibly high heel and stormed back to the elevator, where she had to stop and wait.

Sorry that the interaction had gone so poorly, but immensely glad that the matter was settled, Cole turned back toward his room. He unlocked the door, took off his hat, flung himself onto the very comfortable bed, and picked up the remote control.

Fifteen minutes later, Shawn called. "Maggie just tweeted that you broke up with her."

"What?"

"How do you break up with someone you're not dating?"

"That's a good question. I wasn't dating her, Shawn."

"The tweet says, and I quote, 'Ladies, Cole Washburne isn't the sweetheart he pretends to be. He just dumped me in the hotel hallway.' And then she added several sobbing emojis."

Cole closed his eyes. "Well, sorry, Shawn, but at least it's over."

"We'll see."

32

Lettie arrived to the venue ridiculously early, so she had no trouble finding parking. She looked around in all directions for any sign of Ronnie, but of course, there wasn't any. He probably wasn't going to show. He had probably never left Nashville.

She headed toward the main entrance, where a small crowd was forming. The show was sold out, so she was going to try to buy a ticket on the street. Though she'd never done it before, she thought it would be fairly simple.

Not quite. She quickly spotted a man pacing through the crowd, quietly saying, "Floor tickets for sale" over and over.

She headed his way. "How much for one?" she asked.

He turned to her so quickly his trench coat flared out behind him, making him look like a comic book villain. His upturned collar and dark sunglasses completed the illusion. "Got to take all four, if you want 'em."

She didn't want all four. "How much for all four?"

"Eight hundred."

She cackled. Yeah, right. She wasn't even going to gratify that with a response. She turned and walked away, even though she wasn't sure which direction she should go. There weren't that many people there yet, but the crowd was growing. Eventually, she found another person selling a single ticket, but he wanted five hundred dollars for one. Maybe this wasn't going to work. She continued to wander around, her eyes peeled, her ears keen to hear anything. She told herself as the time got closer, the tickets would get cheaper. If not, she had wasted a trip to Illinois. She found a third man selling tickets, but just as she reached him, he struck a deal with someone else. The crowd continued to grow, and her confidence in her plan shrank accordingly.

The doors opened, and she still didn't have a seat. She re-approached the original villain-scalper, prepared to haggle. He only had two tickets left. He would only sell both. He still wanted eight hundred dollars. She laughed mirthlessly and turned away from him a second time. "I'll take seven hundred!" he called after her. She wanted to punch him in the teeth. Her heart was starting to ache. Had she come all this way for nothing? She'd been so looking forward to seeing Cole, and now it might not happen. She watched the line of people file into the arena, trying to come up with a plan B. Could she sneak in? Did they throw people in jail for that? Her eyes got hot, and she was mortified by the fact that she might soon be in tears over this.

The last of the line disappeared through the door. She looked at her phone. It was seven o'clock. The opening act would be starting any second.

Mr. Trench Coat tapped her on the shoulder, startling her. "I'll give you one for two hundred."

She glared at him. She was so not in the mood for niceties. "I'll give you fifty bucks. Take it or leave it." She knew the tickets had originally cost seventy-five.

He paused, then nodded, almost imperceptibly, and held out his hand.

"Show me the ticket."

He held it out to her. Section D. She might be on the floor, but she wasn't going to be anywhere near the stage. That was okay, though. Hearing Cole drawl on about catching a greased pig wasn't why she'd come to Illinois. She snatched the ticket out of his hand and reached into her pocket. For a second, she panicked that she was going to have to ask this guy to make change, but then she found a ten to complement her two twenties, and she held the money out to him. The exchange happened without further exchange of words, and then she headed for the door.

They had already turned off the house lights, so it was difficult to find her way to her seat, and then once she did, the people in her row refused to let her through. She ended up having to push her way through as if she was in a mosh pit. The image of a country music mosh pit made her giggle as she did so. She was almost there when the crowd erupted in cheers and the stage exploded in lights. Cole must have arrived, but she didn't look up. She took the last eight steps and collapsed into her chair, even though everyone around her was on their feet. Immensely grateful that she had an empty chair beside her, she stood up to realize that a sasquatch with a fifty-gallon hat on his head stood in front of her. Awesome.

Cole began to sing, so at least she could hear him, even if she couldn't see him. He opened with the stupid greased pig song, but when he finished, all of the people around her sat down. Grateful, she followed suit. Some teen girls near the front stayed standing, but they were far enough away to not block her view. And there he was in all his splendor—and her heart galloped at the sight of him. She didn't realize how much she'd missed him until she was looking at him. She realized then that she had very real feelings for him. Maybe it was time to deal with those.

Stop it. That's ridiculous. He's a country singer, for crying out loud.

He sang a slow love song that made her entire body break out in goosebumps. Then he launched into his kit and caboodle song, and the crowd leapt to their feet again. Oh well, she wasn't going to join them this time. She took out her phone and checked for messages. Then she checked the weather. Then she checked Twitter—and saw the break up tweet. Huh. They *had* been together. The thought made her throat close. But they weren't anymore, so that was good. The stupid celebrity drama disgusted her. Real people never moved that fast. She should scoop Cole up to protect him from a lifetime of that—

Stop it. That's ridiculous.

The crowd sat back down, and Cole began a song she hadn't heard before. The first verse was halfway intelligent, but then he started the chorus: "I want you ba-ya-ya-ya-ya-yack," he cried, sounding like a panicked sheep calling out for a yak. She wished she'd brought her noise canceling headphones. Could this get any worse?

And then Maggie Hammer stepped into the spotlight.

33

Cole heard her before he saw her. "I want you ba-ya-ya-ya-ya-yack" she cried, and the crowd went wild. Cole, wondering who had given her a microphone, jumped when she appeared alongside him in the spotlight. The cheers grew even louder. He didn't know if people really loved Maggie Hammer that much, or if they just loved the idea of the two of them together. He looked at her out of the corner of his eye, and she beamed at him. She really was gorgeous. Maybe the fans did love her that much.

And boy, she knew his song. In fact, she was hijacking it. He motioned for her to take the second verse, which she did, seamlessly. He stepped back, allowing her to steal his show, completely aware that the whole thing looked orchestrated. She held her hand out and ran along the edge of the stage, slapping every finger she could reach, which wasn't easy, as security guards stationed along the stage kept the fans from pressing up against it.

She finished the verse, and he joined in on the chorus. They sounded good together. It was too late to cut this as a duet on his album, but maybe they could release it as a single. Maybe the duet could go on *her* album if she ever went solo. And there he was, thinking just like she thought, trying to break up the Hammer Family, which was quite possibly the most talented act in country music. But man, they really did sound good together. That girl could *sing*.

When he entered the bridge, she came and put her hand on his shoulder. He turned toward her without meaning to, and they looked deep into each other's eyes as they both sang into his mic. She started to harmonize with him, and he had to struggle to stick with his own notes and not follow her.

When it was time for the chorus again, he found himself a little dazed. He wasn't feeling anything remotely romantic. It was more like he was enamored by her. He was becoming a fan.

He was *not* a fan of what she did next. The song ended, and before he knew what was happening, she planted her lips on his for all the world to see. He started to pull away, instinctively, but she had a death grip on the front of his shirt, as well as a few of his chest hairs. At the same time, he realized it wouldn't look good if he pushed her off him. So he let her kiss him, but he didn't enjoy it. It felt like being kissed by a mannequin, and it made him wish he was kissing Lettie.

She let go of him, turned to the crowd, waved to them, and then took his hand and led him off stage like a puppy.

The second he was out of the crowd's sight, he grabbed her arm and turned her around to face him. "That was not cool!" he hollered. He wouldn't have hollered at her if it hadn't been so loud.

"Oh, shut up. I advanced your career by *months* if not *years*." She yanked her arm away from his hand, gave him a scalding look, and then walked away from him.

He stood there fuming. He didn't know what else to do. She'd come onto his stage without his permission, without his manager's permission, without *anyone's* permission. How could she get away with that? And what should he do about it?

Shawn appeared deeper backstage and beckoned to him with a finger. Cole headed his way, but before he even got there, Shawn started talking. "I know you're not happy right now, but you should be."

He can't be serious. "I don't think so."

Shawn held his hands up as if trying to calm an angry bull.

Cole pointed at the stage, even though neither of them could see it. "The song was good. I'll give you that, but she doesn't get to treat me like a ... like a ..." Cole didn't know what he wanted to say.

"Like a pawn in her marketing scheme?" Shawn offered.

"Yeah! That!"

Half of Shawn's mouth turned up in a grin. "I'm telling you, it's no big deal."

Cole took a step toward him. He wasn't angry at Shawn, and he tried to remember that as he said, "Can you *please* do something? Talk to her manager, talk to Branch, talk to her mother, I don't care, but I don't want her telling anyone that we're a couple, or doing anything to make people think that."

Shawn nodded. "Okay. I'll do what I can do."

34

Watching the Hammer girl kiss Cole nearly drove Lettie crazy. It made her feel hot all over and sick to her stomach. Still, as soon as they left the stage, she made her way to the front. She had no idea how to get backstage, despite the fact that she'd spent much of her childhood backstage, albeit in back of much smaller stages.

She approached the first security guy she saw. There was no music, but she still had to raise her voice to drown out the crowd. "I'm a friend of Cole Washburne's." She pointed to her own ear to indicate his ear piece. "Can you tell someone to tell him I'm here?"

The man said nothing, just shook his head.

She was afraid that might happen. "It's really important. I need to warn him about something."

The man furrowed his brow a little and appeared to be considering her request, but he still didn't do anything.

She gave him a second to think, but she knew the Hammer Family would be on the stage soon, and then he wouldn't be able to hear her. "Can you ask your boss or something?"

"Go back to your seat, ma'am," he said in a tone several shades past rude.

Ugh. She turned and started the long walk out of the auditorium. She'd just reached the doors to the lobby when she heard the Hammer Family take the stage. The doors closed behind her, and gratitude washed over her. The relative quiet was so wonderful. She hooked away from the front doors and headed down a wide hallway that circled the auditorium. It didn't take her long to encounter more security guards. "Hi!" she said, trying to sound sane and cheery. "I'm a friend of Cole Washburne's. Can you ask one of his people to tell him that I'm here?"

The men looked at each other and chuckled. "Sorry, no admittance past this point," one of them said in a monotone.

No kidding. "Yeah, I know that. I'm not trying to walk by you," she said slowly. "I'm asking you to contact someone who will let him know I'm here. I really need to talk to him."

"You should call him," the other man said. Then they laughed.

Oh, these guys were really annoying.

"You're missing the show, ma'am."

Like she gave two shakes about a stupid music show. "Look, it's kind of a long story, but I'm telling you. It's really important. There's this man, and I don't know much about him, but he sort of threatened Cole, and I just want to warn him—"

"Threatened him how?" the first man asked, his body coming to attention.

"He didn't really. He just said some weird stuff, and I don't know what he meant, but he might be coming here."

The man's body relaxed. He had already decided to dismiss her. "Well, if he tries to come through here, we'll stop him, just like we're stopping you."

She gave up then. "Can you just pass on the message, then? Tell Cole's people that a guy claiming to be Lettie's father might be coming to harass Cole?"

He nodded. "Sure."

He was going to do no such thing, and she knew it. She could see his buddy biting back a laugh.

"Okay, fine. I'm leaving. And I hope nothing happens. But if it does, I'll be sure to let Cole know that you didn't warn him."

Something resembling doubt flickered across the second man's face, but it wasn't enough. They remained rooted to their spots. There was no point. So she headed for the doors with no idea what she was going to do when she got there. This was the stupidest fifty bucks she'd ever spent. She had no interest in watching the rest of the show. She went and sat in her car, feeling defeated.

Now what? Should she just go home? No, she wasn't going to give up, not now that she'd come this far. He was playing in Moline again tomorrow night. That gave her twenty-four hours to come up with a better plan. She needed to find a cheap hotel. She started her car and pulled it out into traffic. She had gone by some hotels on her way to the center; she was sure she could find her way back.

She was wrong. Within a few minutes of focusing more on Cole's duet with Maggie than on where she was driving, she was all turned around and had no idea which way was which. They'd seemed awfully comfortable together, and Lettie hadn't liked the look of that. She needed to find somewhere to park so she could use her phone to find a hotel. As she looked for a safe place to pull over, she saw a giant, black bus with tinted windows.

Could that be it? Could that be him? Who else could it be? It wasn't the Hammer Family or Branch. It really might be Cole. She gunned the engine, took a hard right turn, and followed the bus. There were two cars between her and him, and she stayed right on the first one's bumper. So, she almost had an embarrassing moment when that car stopped to let a woman cross the road. Shoot! No time for niceties right now. She saw the bus turn left while she was still sitting there, stopped behind the crosswalk, and panicked. After all this, she wasn't going to lose him now. But the car in front of her was still stopped, now waiting for a man and his dog to cross. The dog appeared to be a hundred and five years old and was walking so slowly that he was barely moving. This wasn't working.

She looked in her rearview mirror, saw she had a few feet to spare, threw her car in reverse, and backed up. Then she put it in drive and yanked her wheel to the right. Her right tire bumped up onto the curb, jerking her neck out of alignment. The right back tire followed up as the front tire came crashing back down to the street, and she was free.

The back tire came down, slamming her spine back into alignment, and she gave it some gas. She floored it, took the left the bus had taken, and then—nothing.

There was no bus anywhere in sight.

She was back to zero.

She considered checking every hotel parking lot in the city, but she figured some of them—especially the ones that fancy pants country stars used—had garages. She was sunk. Again. She drove around a few blocks, thinking she might get lucky, but she didn't, of course. She found a cheap chain motel and pulled into the empty lot. Twenty minutes and sixty dollars later, she was checking under the bed for dead bodies. Finding none, she settled down on the bed and started searching for pizza joints that would deliver.

Then she had a better idea. In fact, the entire plan formed in her head in a single second, and it seemed so brilliant, she was embarrassed she hadn't thought of it for the first concert. It would work. She knew it. She just needed a few supplies. It was time to go to Walmart.

35

Cole was up bright and early for another radio interview. The opportunity cheered him up immensely. One of Branch's security guys drove him to the radio station and then walked him inside, even though there was no one to protect him from. Most of Moline was still sleeping.

"Welcome!" a portly man said as he pumped Cole's hand up and down. "Have a seat!"

Cole set his guitar case down and sat in the chair the man had pointed to.

"Name's Jorry Laner. It's a real pleasure, Cole. I'm a big fan."

Cole smiled broadly. The man seemed so sincere. He tipped his hat to him. "Much obliged, Jorry, and the pleasure's all mine." He motioned toward his guitar case. "You mind if I tune up?"

"No, be my guest. We'll go on the air in just a few minutes. Until then, do what you got to do. Would you like some coffee?"

"That'd be great, thanks. Extra cream, if you've got it."

"Coming right up." Jorry vanished into the next room, and Cole unpacked his guitar. It didn't take long, and he was all tuned up by the time Jorry reappeared with a Styrofoam cup. He set it in front of Cole, and the coffee sloshed out onto the table. Jorry didn't seem to mind. He sat down on the other side of the small room and adjusted his microphone. Cole looked around for a napkin, but didn't see any. He picked up the coffee and took a sip. It was terrible and burned the roof of his mouth, but he took a second sip just the same.

Jorry pointed to a pair of headphones that lay on the table beside Cole. "When you're ready, get suited up." He laughed at his own joke, and his neck jiggled.

Cole put the headphones on.

"Good morning, Quad Cities!" Jorry said into his microphone. "This is Jorry Laner at your service, and I'm here this morning with up-and-coming country music sensation Cole Washburne! Good morning, Cole."

Cole's belly rolled with unexpected nerves. He'd done this before, of course, but it wasn't lost on him how many people could be listening. And there were no edits on live radio. "Good morning, Jorry. And thank you for your kind words."

"You're welcome. So, what's it like being on tour with Branch Bronson?"

"Oh, you know, he's the absolute best. I couldn't ask for a better headliner. I love his music, and I'm learning a lot from him."

"That's great, Cole. We've got lots of Branch fans around here. So, what's it like watching your first single tearing up the charts?"

Cole's smile was so wide he felt foolish. "It's the best feeling in the world, Jorry. Feels like all my dreams are coming true."

"And do those dreams include Miss Maggie Hammer?"

Cole's smile dropped off his face in an instant. He had no idea what to say to that, and his hesitation felt long. "Maggie and I are just friends."

Jorry laughed, putting his hand on his belly as if it hurt to laugh that hard.

Cole found the sound of his laughter patronizing.

"You looked like more than friends on the stage last night."

Oddly, an image of Lettie popped into Cole's mind. Where had that come from? He tried to focus. "Yeah, I'm sure we did. But I assure you, and everyone, that there's nothing romantic going on with Maggie and me." As he talked, he grew more and more angry with Maggie. What had she gotten him into? "You know, Maggie is a real talented performer, and ..."

Jorry's eyes widened, and he leaned closer to the mic. "Are you saying the kiss was part of the performance?"

Oh, why not throw her under the bus? She'd driven the bus right over him. "Yeah, that's what I'm saying."

Jorry looked as though he'd just uncovered the juiciest scandal of his career. "Well, you heard it here first, friends. That's what I call really getting into a song! Stay tuned through this short break, and when we come back, Cole's going to sing us his new single." Jorry pushed the mic away and took off his headphones. He looked at Cole. "If I were you, I'd wanna spend some more time on stage with her." He laughed again. He found himself hilarious. "You're on in sixty seconds."

36

Lettie pulled the covers up over her head. She didn't want to be awake yet. She had nothing to do all day and wanted to squeeze every cent out of her room's rate. She'd check out at exactly eleven o'clock, not a second sooner. The room was chilly. She'd slept with the windows open to try to get the smell of spray paint out of the room. A quick sniff told her she hadn't been completely successful.

Long before eleven, hunger interfered with Lettie's plan to sleep in, and she grudgingly crawled out of bed to go search for a store that sold Pop-Tarts. She quickly found one, and got herself a large coffee, a pair of frosted strawberry tarts, and a package of Ho Hos for dessert.

The second Moline show wasn't sold out, so Lettie didn't have to go to ridiculous measures to procure a ticket. She just ordered one online like a normal person. Fortunately, there were floor seats left. Unfortunately, the floor seats cost three times as much as the nosebleed seats. Still, it was worth it. For her new plan, she'd need to be close to the stage.

After breakfast, she settled back onto the bed and picked up the remote.

She watched television till eleven and then checked out. Then she sat in her car for a while wondering what to do next. What was there to do in Moline, exactly? She didn't have much money left. A quick internet search told her, however, that if she skipped over to Iowa, there was a giant Center for the Arts to explore. So, she headed that way. She didn't think she'd ever been to Iowa either, though, with her childhood, who knew? It occurred to her she could ask her brother, but if he *ever* found out what she was doing right now, stalking a country music star to try to save him from a potential stalker, Darren would never let her live it down.

The Center for the Arts was just what she needed. Gallery after gallery of paintings, photos, sculptures, and even jewelry. Some of the art made her laugh out loud. Some made her eyes water with tears she didn't let fall. And some she just plain didn't understand. She wished she had more artistic talent. Wouldn't it be great to be able to express yourself like this? She vowed to find a pottery class when she got home.

Her hours in the art center reinforced her belief that she and Cole couldn't possibly work together. He would never enjoy this. She'd only seen one cowboy depicted in the entire building. But that was okay. She didn't need to be Cole's girlfriend. She still wanted to be his friend. And even if that wasn't possible, she still needed to warn him about Ronnie.

After a fast food supper that made her drowsy, it was time to head for the venue. She wanted to get there early so she could get good parking.

And she did. She found herself near the front of the line this time with ticket and paraphernalia in hand. A few people gave her armload a strange look, but no one said anything.

Until security, anyway. The doors opened, and she made her way through them, but then she was stopped. A friendly face told her she couldn't take the sticks inside. They weren't *sticks*—they were *mop handles*—and she had paid a pretty penny for them. "Why not?" she asked, realizing too late that her sassy tone probably wouldn't help her cause.

"You could bludgeon someone with one of those," the friendly guard said.

"But how am I supposed to hold my sign up?"

The guard shrugged. That wasn't his problem. "You can leave your sign here or you can go put it back in your vehicle, but we've got to keep the line moving."

"Fine," she said, ripping off the duct tape, "but I'm not leaving the sign. You can have the *sticks*." She tore the king-sized sheet off the mop handles, balled it up under her arm with half of the silver tape still attached, and turned to go into the arena.

"Love the pink," the guard called after her.

At first she thought he meant her hair, but then she realized he was referring to her bedding. "It was the only color they had," she called back. This wasn't true, of course, but pink had been the *cheapest*. And she could see why. It wasn't pink so much as a pale salmon, but it didn't matter. It would do the trick—at least, she hoped it still would, without her mop handles.

She found her seat and then waited patiently, nervously, with the salmon sheet in her lap. Her seat looked farther from the stage than it had on the online seating chart. She was twenty rows deep. A long strip of stage ran out into the center of the crowd, and she was ten seats to the right of that. If she remembered correctly, Cole had only sauntered down that center strip once, though she could have missed a second or third trip, as she'd spent some of the time in her seat sulking. Not tonight, though. This was her last chance. Do or die. She was not going to follow him to the next city.

After what felt like forever, the house lights dimmed, and the swelling crowd got louder. Lots of seats around her were empty. Tonight hadn't sold out. Or maybe people didn't care about the opening act and were just planning on getting there for the headliner.

Cole stepped out onto the stage, and her heart jumped into her throat. The man was beautiful. Even if he did wear a cowboy hat. His smile a mile wide, he stepped up the microphone. A sudden terror overwhelmed her. What was she doing? This wasn't going to work! She was going to make a fool of herself. She squeezed her eyes shut and pictured Cole without the spotlight, without the stupid hat. She saw him sitting on her couch, his blond curls spilling onto his forehead.

Just do it. She leaned back and reached behind two people to tap the shoulder of a good-looking guy in flannel.

He looked at her, obviously already annoyed.

"Please hold this," she hollered, pushing the corner of a sheet to him.

He scowled, shook his head, and looked back at the stage.

She had anticipated this. She poked him harder, maybe *too* hard even. Her shiny black fingernail sunk into his shoulder further than she'd meant for it to. He glared at her.

"Do it!" she hollered and handed him a twenty.

She wasn't sure if it was the twenty or his bewilderment, but he took the corner of the sheet. Then he looked at her as if to say, "What now?"

She hopped up onto her chair and nodded toward his chair for him to do the same. He looked horrified, but he did it. She was going to have to give him a big thank you later.

And just like that—the salmon sheet was in the air. She didn't think Cole would be able to see the whole sign without the help of the mop handles, no matter how high she stretched her arm. The bottom of her message was draped over her feet. She scrunched up the top of the sheet, surely obscuring the top of the message, but that was okay. It just said, "Cole." He could probably ascertain whom the message was for without that salutation.

The people behind her started hollering at her and her new flannel-clad friend, and she was a little worried he would crumble under the pressure. Couldn't they just wait a second? She wasn't going to do this for the whole show. She just needed to make sure Cole saw the sheet. The person behind her pulled down on her shirt—hard.

She whirled around to glare at him, almost losing her balance and toppling into the row in front of her. "Just a minute!" she screamed. Gosh, these people would never make it at a Pearl Jam concert if they were this upset about her salmon sheet. She looked forward and peeked around the edge of her sheet as Cole began a second song. He wasn't looking in her direction, but he was coming down the little strip of stage. She tried to turn her body, so that he'd still be able to see the sign. As she turned, the man behind her pushed her forward, and this time she did fall. She slammed into the man in front of her, bounced back into her own row, and then scrambled back up into her chair, but as she did so, she saw a large security guard coming down the aisle with his eyes on her. Shoot! Without thinking, she started to do the vine down the row of chairs, getting closer to Cole and further from Mr. Security. At first, Mr. Flannel didn't follow her, and she yanked on the sheet to signal to him that he should. Of course, he just let go of the sheet, and she staggered to the left with his sudden release. The salmon sheet fell onto the heads of the people in her row and she hurried to pull it off them, throwing herself even more off balance until she was sure she was going to fall all the way to the left with a mighty crash. Her feet scrambled to try to prevent this from happening, but the faster her feet moved across the chairs, the faster she lost her balance. She knew she was going to fall. She knew it was going to hurt. She knew the chairs would never hold her. She was going all the way to the floor. She might die. And there was nothing she could do to save herself.

37

Cole saw it happening before he realized it was Lettie. Some lunatic was almost completely cocooned in an ugly pink sheet and half-running, half-falling down the row of chairs toward him. He didn't know whether to laugh or be scared for his safety. Then he saw the pink hair peeking out of the cocoon and he knew. A desperate protectiveness filled him, and he stopped singing and pointed. "Y'all want to help her?" he said into the microphone and hurried to the edge of the stage. He got there just as she did and caught her by one of her shoulders. Amazingly, the people in her row caught the rest of her, and helped push her up onto the stage, where she lay, wrapped up like a pink mummy. What on earth? She scrambled to free herself from her shroud and came up onto one knee. Then she looked around wide-eyed, as if she'd just realized she was on stage. She looked up at him and mumbled something, which of course, he couldn't hear. He reached down and pulled her to her feet, taking care to hold the microphone down by his leg. "What?" he shouted.

The fans were screaming as if they knew who this was and they'd just been on the edge of their seats waiting for her to arrive.

"I have to talk to you!" Lettie hollered into his face.

Well, obviously. "Okay, go backstage." He pointed. "I'll be right there." She nodded, and he almost laughed. He'd never seen her look so serious. She started to walk away from him, then came back and hurriedly picked up her sheet, and then ran off stage. He looked out at Branch's fans. "Sorry about that, y'all. That was a friend of mine, and well"—he looked over his shoulder—"well, the truth is, I'm not really sure what that was, but let's get back to the music."

Blessedly, his band picked back up, and he started to sing again.

WHEN COLE GOT BACKSTAGE, he found Lettie surrounded by security—both Branch's and the venue's. He waved them off. "It's okay, it's okay. She's my friend."

"We still don't let friends climb onstage," Branch's guy Reynold said.

"It won't happen again," Lettie said meekly, as if she'd already said this a few times. "It was important."

"Okay?" Cole looked at the black-clad men. "Can we just give her a warning and let it go?"

Everyone looked to Reynold, who finally nodded.

"Great, then. Lettie, let's go find someplace quiet." He reached for her hand, and when she gave it to him, fireworks erupted in his chest. Oh wowsa, he'd missed her.

He led her to his dressing room, and they sat down on a small couch. He couldn't believe how happy he was to be so close to her. "So, to what do I owe the honor?" he asked and then laughed.

"Well, I know you said you always wanted someone to wrap themselves in pink and then fall onto your stage." She laughed too and put her head in her hands. "I'm so sorry. I'm so embarrassed. But I lost your number, and I couldn't call you, and I tried to tweet Maggie, but she blocked me." She looked up at him. "I take it she didn't give you the message?"

Oh great. Let's involve Maggie. He shook his head. "What message?"

"Same one that was on the sheet."

He laughed. "What was on the sheet?"

She stared at him for a moment, as if she didn't understand. Then she slowly unfurled the pink cloth she'd been clutching, to reveal the large black letters that said, "COLE, CALL LETTIE!"

He laughed. "You lost my number?" That didn't make sense. Had she lost her phone?

She nodded, keeping her eyes on the sheet. "Sort of."

She sort of lost his number? What did that mean? He decided to let that one go, for now. "Okay, so why did you want me to call you?"

She looked at him then. "So this guy came into Maxwell's, and he says he's my father." She stopped for a second, giving him time to absorb that.

"Okay," he said, urging her to go on.

Then her words spilled out rapidly. "I don't think he really is, I don't care if he really is, and I let him know that, but then he got all shady, and he sort of threatened you, and he might not be dangerous at all, I don't know, but if he is, then I had to come warn you." She took a quick breath. "Sorry."

He put his hand on her back and rubbed gently. It felt so good to touch her. He felt himself relax at the contact. "No need to be sorry. I appreciate you coming all this way to warn me." He paused, wondering how to phrase the question he wanted to ask. "But now that you've come all this way, want to stick around a while?"

She smiled up at him. He could see thoughts racing behind her eyes. He wished he could quiet her mind for a while.

"Maybe."

"Yeah? You know, the job offer still stands."

The smile left her face.

"I mean, or you could just tag along for a few days," he hurried to say.

"Maybe," she said again. A mischievous light sparked in her eyes. "I should probably join your security team. I'm the one who knows what your potential assailant looks like."

He wanted to kiss her. She was so cute. But he didn't. "Deal."

"What am I going to do with my car?"

Oh shoot, he hadn't thought of that. "You can drive it behind the bus if you want, but it might be easier to drive it into the river and report it stolen."

She laughed, and the sound of it made his heart dance.

38

Lettie drove toward the used car dealership, trying to keep her eyes on the road, when they kept trying to drift toward the man in the passenger seat. Stupid eyes.

The tour had a night off, so even though the rest of the busses set sail for Indianapolis, Cole had his bus stay behind so that he could help Lettie sell her car. When he'd suggested the idea, he'd acted as if she'd balk at it, but she hadn't. She sorely needed a cash influx if she was going to continue this new nomad lifestyle. She figured Cole would pay her eventually, as he was her boss now, but she didn't want to ask her new boss for an advance.

Besides, her car was a hunk of junk.

Cole would be returning to Nashville in a few days. He had to get back for his album launch party, and he said she could go back with him and get anything from home that she needed. She wouldn't need much. She liked to travel light.

Shawn hadn't even laughed when Cole told him that Lettie was going to be the inaugural member of his security team. "Eventually, I'll have her in charge of them all. But right now, I thought it would be good to keep her on the payroll, as she knows what the guy looks like." He'd made it sound so logical, even though Lettie found it absurd. If Shawn had found it absurd, his face didn't betray that.

And so now she had a new job. She'd already called Max, who hadn't sounded surprised—or as sad as she thought he'd be. And now they were driving to some used car dealer Cole had found online. He'd made an appointment, so a short smiley man named Andrew met them in the parking lot.

"Is this it?" He looked at the car, not even trying to hide his disappointment.

Lettie's shoulders rolled back. Her old Mazda wasn't much, but it still deserved some respect.

"Yep." Cole patted the roof as if it were an old dog. "This is it."

"And you have the title?"

Why did he sound so skeptical? "Yes," Lettie said. That was a stroke of luck. She'd only recently paid off the car, and when the title had come in the mail, she'd just shoved it into the glove compartment.

"And how much were you hoping to get for it?"

Cole shrugged. "Just want a fair price."

Andrew walked around the car, looking it over carefully. He stopped in front of the hood and scratched his chin. "I can give you three hundred."

Sold, Lettie thought.

"Three hundred?" Cole cried. "Don't act like you're going to scrap it. You could sell this car. It runs great."

That's a small exaggeration, Lettie thought, but she didn't want to interrupt.

Andrew didn't look surprised by Cole's response. "Well, we don't usually resell cars this old."

A quick glance around the lot told Lettie otherwise, but again, she chose silence.

Cole stayed quiet.

"I could do five."

"You can do eight," Cole said quickly, matter-of-factly. Why was he so good at this?

Andrew sighed, put his hand on his hip, looked down at the car again, though Lettie thought he was avoiding Cole's gaze more than he was examining the hood. "Seven. Final offer."

Cole looked at her for approval, which, of course, she quickly gave. She'd been ready to let it go for three. Cole looked at Andrew. "It's a deal."

"Great." Andrew didn't sound like he thought it was great. "I'll go draw up the paperwork. Come on inside when you're ready."

Cole watched him walk to the door and then looked at Lettie. "Do you want a minute alone for a last goodbye?"

How thoughtful of him. "Nah, it's just a hunk of metal." This in no way matched how she really felt. In reality, she was on the verge of tears saying goodbye to this old friend whom she'd cursed so often for not doing what she wanted it to do when she wanted it to do it. But she didn't want Cole to know she was emotionally attached to a car. She already feared he thought she was crazy after the whole bedding on stage incident.

"All right, then. You want to go inside?"

She nodded, and he put his arm around her shoulders and led her toward the door. The gesture was both intimate and friendly, and it confused her. Just how did Cole feel about her now? Was she just an employee? And did it even matter how he felt?

Cole took his hat off, and they settled into some plastic chairs that were more comfortable than they looked and waited. She had a crazy urge to run her fingers through his hair, which she ignored. Cole caught her staring at his locks. "What?"

She forced her eyes away. "Nothing. I was just thinking again that you look better without your hat on."

His cheeks got pink.

"So that's some duet you and Maggie Hammer have got going." She was just trying to move the conversation away from his discomfort, but as soon as she'd spoken the words, she realized she might have sounded a little jealous, and she looked at the floor to hide her own burning cheeks.

Cole grunted. "No. Maggie Hammer and I have *nothing* going."

"What?" She tried to look at him without lifting her head.

He leaned back in his chair and sighed. "She came out on stage and hijacked my song. That's sort of how she operates—hijacking things. She's kind of driving me nuts." He smiled down at her, and she finally lifted her head to meet his gaze. She couldn't not. "Maggie's got some issues, and I'm going to try to keep my distance so I don't get further sucked into her drama."

He'd been dating her only days ago, and now he was talking about her like this? Not cool. "But you were just dating her."

He shook his head slowly. "No, I wasn't. She lied, plain and simple. I don't know what she was thinking exactly, but I guess she thought her fans would like it if we were a thing."

Lettie's mouth dropped open. "What? She wanted to be your fake girlfriend? But I thought I was your fake girlfriend!" She leaned into him playfully, and when she bounced off him, she wished she'd just stayed leaning on him.

He chuckled. "Yeah, that fake relationship was way more fun." He turned toward her suddenly. His hands fiddled with the hat in his hands, but his eyes were rock steady. "You know, you could be my real girl—"

"All right," Andrew interrupted. "If you come right this way, we'll get your signature and give you a check."

39

Cole couldn't sit still, and his increasingly more crowded tour bus had no room for nervous pacing. To distract himself, he'd binged on junk food, and now he had a stomachache to complement the stomach rolls Lettie's presence was giving him.

It was less than five hours to Indianapolis. It felt like so much longer.

For the first hour, he tried to convince himself that what he was feeling for Lettie wasn't love. But if it *wasn't* love, then what *was* it? He couldn't decide. He'd never felt like this about any woman. But she was so *not* what he'd planned on. He couldn't really see a future with her. Wait, that wasn't true. He *could* see a future with her. It just wasn't the future he'd spent his whole life envisioning: the music career, the cute ranch, the blond wife who prided herself on homemaking and cooking, the many kids spilling out of the house when he got home from tour—would Lettie even *want* children? And did she even know how to cook anything? The woman lived on Ho Hos for crying out loud.

He couldn't take his eyes off her. She sat looking out the window, watching the world whiz by, with earbuds tucked into her cute little ears. She looked so content there, on his bus, on a *country music tour.* Encouraged to see her listening to music, he sat down in the seat facing her and smiled.

She didn't return his smile as she took out an earbud. He got the impression she hadn't wanted to be interrupted.

"Sorry, didn't mean to disturb you."

"No, that's okay. It was just a really good part. What's up?"

A good part? Like a rousing bridge? "Who are you listening to?"

She gave him a wry smile then. "I don't know the narrator's name, but I'm listening to an audiobook."

"Oh." He had no idea what to say to that. After some fumbling, he asked, "What's it about?"

"A vampire ventriloquist."

He laughed. Wait, was she kidding? He couldn't tell. A smile played around her eyes, but he didn't know why she was smiling. Out of fondness for the vampire? Because she enjoyed his discomfort? Or because she was messing with him? "Seriously?"

She nodded. "Want to join me?" She held one of her earbuds out to him.

He so did not want to listen to a story about a vampire ventriloquist. "Sure." He slid out of his seat and into hers, delighting at the feel of her warm shoulder against his. He took the earbud and put it in his ear, suddenly panicking because he couldn't remember the last time he'd cleaned out his ears. He slid down in the seat, folded his hands, and began to listen. The vampire was picking out a new dummy. Or maybe a new victim. He couldn't tell. He also didn't care, and his mind began to wander.

It was time to admit it. He was in love with Lettie. As he consciously opened his heart to accept this reality, a warmth filled him all the way to his toes. It didn't matter what he'd planned for his life—she was the new plan. And this idea thrilled him. He couldn't wait to build a life with her. She could be head of his security team. They could bring the kids on tour. He looked at her out of the corner of his eye. She'd returned her gaze to the window. *If* she wanted a life like that. *If* she wanted *him*. The truth was, he had no idea what she wanted. She'd never mentioned a plan or a dream. She'd seemed content to just ride along through life as a server in a bar.

He looked down at the tattoo on her arm and before he realized what he was doing, he reached out and caressed it.

She jumped and looked at him, her eyebrows raised in question.

"Sorry." And he was. Sorry *and* embarrassed. "Just wondering what this meant." It was a colorful butterfly made up of puzzle pieces. A few of the pieces sat off to the side, as if the puzzle had been abandoned.

She rolled her eyes. "Tattoos don't have to have meaning."

"Oh." Why would anyone subject themselves to that much pain if there was no meaning attached? "So this one doesn't? Have any meaning, I mean." He wished he'd kept his mouth shut.

She smiled. "It does. It means that if I want to fly, I need to put the pieces together."

His breath caught. "Wowsa. That's awesome. It would make a good song."

She rolled her eyes again and pressed play on the audiobook. The deep man's voice came back to life in his ear, startling him. "Make up your own songs," she said, but half of her mouth was curled up in a smile. She looked out the window again.

He wanted to help her put the puzzle pieces together. He also wanted to write a song about that. Could he spend the rest of his life in a love he wasn't allowed to write about? He'd have to negotiate that part. *If* she was even interested in negotiating. He had to tell her how he felt. But how? Of course, the simplest answer was the one that wouldn't possibly work: write a song for her. He tried to think of another option. He'd confessed love before, to several women, even though he'd never felt for them like he felt for Lettie. And it had come out easier then. There was too much at stake now. With the other women, his heart had been in danger of disappointment and embarrassment. Now his heart was in danger of being shattered. He racked his brain. Flowers? Did Lettie even *like* roses? He scanned her skin for evidence. Yep, she had a few small roses near her elbow. But they were black. Should he get her *black* roses? The idea made him laugh.

She looked at him. "You find that funny?"

He found what funny? Oh no, what had just happened in the stupid vampire book he was listening to? He paid attention to the words for the first time, and it sounded like someone was being chased up a fire escape. "No, no, not funny. Sorry, I was thinking about something else."

Looking relieved, she turned her eyes back to the window.

Maybe he should get a tattoo. Yeah! That was it! It would hurt like the dickens, but he could do it, right? Lots of people got tattoos. He'd have to put it somewhere his mother wouldn't see it; she'd have a heart attack if she knew. But he would do it. Lettie would love it. He was so excited to have figured it out. He unlocked his phone screen to search for tattoo parlors in Indianapolis. An overwhelming number of options appeared. This many people got tattoos? He modified his search: reputable, clean, safe tattoo parlors in Indianapolis. The same number of results appeared, but somehow he still felt better.

40

The bus pulled into Indianapolis hours before they needed to be at the arena. Lettie panicked a little, wondering what she was going to do with her free time. She had no car. Was she going to be trapped on a tour bus?

Though Cole gave her no reason to think he was aware of her anxiety, he quickly assuaged her fears. He held his arm out to her. "If you would like to accompany me, I've got a spectacular plan for the next few hours." His voice wavered a little. Was he nervous about something?

"Like what?" She was going to go along with whatever he had cooked up, of course, but she didn't want to appear overeager. She did, however, take his arm, and the firmness of it beneath her fingers made her feel all squishy inside. Of course, she would die before she would let him know this.

"I planned a Lettie day."

She barked out a laugh. "You *what*?" Why would he do that?

"Yep, with the help of Google, I have designed a day especially for you. So let's go. The cab will be here any second."

"Um ... okay." She groped around for her bag, which was right beside her, but she still had immense trouble locating it and then putting its strap over her shoulder. She then followed him, still holding onto his arm, off the bus.

The cab wasn't there yet. "Tell me where we're going."

"You'll see."

When the cab did arrive, Cole opened the door for her, and gave the driver an address instead of a location name, so she still had no clue. The driver gave no reaction to the address. She took this as encouraging. If Cole had said something too bizarre, the driver would have reacted, right? She hoped so.

Ten minutes later, the taxi pulled into the parking lot of what looked like a cross between a factory and a school. "What *is* this place?" Then she saw the sign, which was oddly small for the size of the building: Hostess Cake. "Um, Cole, really, what are we doing?"

"We're getting you some Ho Hos. And they're going to be fresh." He handed the driver some cash. "Keep the change." Then he climbed out of the car.

She followed his lead. They were at a Ho Ho factory? Really? She was partly bewildered, partly ecstatic.

He took her by the hand. "Branch pulled some strings. The manager is a fan."

She laughed then, a high-pitched giggle that embarrassed her. She clapped her free hand over her mouth. "They let people in?"

"I'm not sure if they let *people* in, but they're letting *us* in." He smiled down at her. "Sometimes it pays to be a rising star." He started walking toward the door, and she fell into step with him.

"Just imagine when you're no longer rising, and *you're* the big star. You won't need Branch to pull strings."

He beamed.

She didn't know what she'd said to make him so happy, but she realized then that making him happy made *her* happy—very.

They could smell the sweetness before they even got to the door, and when Cole opened the door for her, the smell wafted over them, and she was suddenly starving. A woman with a plastic cap over her hair greeted them with a broad smile. "Welcome! Welcome! We're so glad to have you! I'm Elvie." She stuck out her hand, and they each shook it in turn.

"Lettie," she offered.

"Cole." He tipped his hat.

"Pleasure to meet you. I'm a huge country music fan." She handed them each a plastic cap. "Sorry, it's the rules."

Lettie didn't mind, but Cole looked as though he did. He grudgingly took off his hat, slid the plastic on over his curls, and then put the hat back on. He nodded at the woman to signal that he was ready.

"Great! Right this way!" She led them through large swinging doors, and the smell grew even stronger, which Lettie wouldn't have thought possible thirty seconds ago. It was overwhelming. *If I worked here, I would either get fired for pilfering or lose my taste for the treats altogether.*

Cole took her hand again, and she was glad for it. Her heart swelled with affection for the man she had nothing in common with. *Careful, Lettie,* an annoying voice in her head warned her. She ignored it. She was going to enjoy this day for all it was worth. Caution could wait till the next city.

A giant conveyor belt stood before them, and it was covered in chocolaty dough. She gasped.

Elvie laughed. "Yep, this is where it begins." She pointed to a large hopper. "We mix the ingredients, and then pour them onto the belt, and then we bake them." She began to walk down the conveyor, which was *loud*. The chocolate cake didn't really look like food at this point. Once it was cooked, a row of dispensers squirted the cream out onto the cake, and her mouth watered. Then a row of sticks spun the cake and frosting up into a row. The whole thing looked so complicated to her—futuristic even. Yet the few employees in the room stood around looking bored, as if they didn't have to do anything unless something went wrong. If she worked there, she'd hope for things to go wrong so she could take the mistakes home with her. The belt now held three Ho Hos that were about twenty feet long. It was the most beautiful thing she'd ever seen. Disappointed, she watched a new machine cut them into familiarly sized pieces.

The belt curved, and they hustled to keep up. She sneaked a look at Cole, and his smile stretched from ear to ear. She didn't think she'd ever seen him look so gleeful. Maybe he loved Ho Hos more than he'd let on. They kept walking, as the Ho Hos lined up single file and zipped through a new contraption. When they came out on the other side, they were neatly wrapped in plastic.

Elvie stood there staring at the scene for a few minutes and then led them out into a hallway. As the door shut behind them, the noise cut off, and it seemed eerily quiet. "And there you have it! The birth of Ho Hos!" She laughed. "Do you have any questions?"

"Yes," Lettie said quickly.

Elvie and Cole both looked at her expectantly.

"Do you have any I could eat?"

Elvie laughed again and didn't look even remotely surprised. "Absolutely, right this way." She led them into a break room. A few white-clad employees stood up and left when they entered, making Lettie feel bad. Elvie reached into a box and grabbed two handfuls of Ho Hos, which she then offered to Lettie. "These are seconds, but they taste like firsts."

Lettie accepted them with gratitude. She wanted to rip into one of the packages right then, but she was embarrassed enough to show restraint. "Thank you so much." She held up her full hands. "For these, and for the tour."

"You bet. Is there anything else you want to see?"

Lettie didn't know what to say. She could have happily stayed there all day. She looked at Cole.

He looked down at her as he answered Elvie. "Actually, we've got another stop to make, but thank you so much for your hospitality."

"Sure thing! I'll show you out." Without looking to see if they would follow, she headed through the door and down a long hallway.

They did follow, of course, even though Lettie didn't really want to. She took off her plastic cap along the way, and when, after they had said their goodbyes and stepped outside into the sunshine, Cole didn't take his off, she motioned to his head. "As good as that looks, it might get hot."

At first, he didn't understand. Then he jumped and took it off as fast as he could, shoving the thing into the pocket of his tight jeans. She caught herself examining the tightness of those jeans and forced herself to look at his face. "Now what? You said we had another stop to make."

"Yes, Lettie." Without saying more, he took out his phone and called for another cab. Then he looked at her. "I am going to get my first tattoo, and I was hoping you'd come along for emotional support."

She could have been knocked over with a feather. Cole with a tattoo? No way! She must be having more of an influence on him than she thought.

He chuckled nervously. "Let's walk toward the road while we wait for the cab." He took her hand.

They started walking. "What brought this on?"

He looked out at the road and shrugged. "Well, actually, I wanted to tell you something, and getting that something tattooed onto my skin seemed like the best way to say it."

What? That didn't even make sense. "Or you could just tell me—"

A cab whipped into the parking lot, and Lettie assumed it was theirs.

It wasn't. The back door of the car opened, and a denim-clad Ronnie climbed out of the car.

Lettie's stomach rolled, and she clenched at Cole's hand.

"What? What is it? Are you okay?"

"That's him," she said and her own voice sounded weak. "That's him," she said again, sounding stronger. "The guy who says he's my father."

"Well, hello, Cole Washburne!" Ronnie stuck out his hand. "So good to meet you! I'm a big fan!"

Cole accepted his handshake. "Good to meet you too, sir. What can we do for you?"

Ronnie's smile flickered. "Do for me? Nothing. I just wanted to get to know the man who is hooking up with my daughter."

Lettie started to sweat. Hooking up? What a creep!

"So you came all the way to Indianapolis?" Cole's words were clipped, his tone sarcastic.

Ronnie stepped back and folded his arms across his chest. "Well, I thought I'd catch the show. Figured you could get me backstage."

Lettie found her voice. "How did you find us?"

He shrugged. "Roommate told me where you'd gone. I looked up the tour schedule, and then some kid with the tour told me you'd come here, once I'd explained that I was your dad." He glanced at the factory. "Can't imagine why you're here, but I didn't want to let the grass grow under my feet." He stepped toward her and slapped her on the shoulder just a little too hard.

Cole let go of her hand and put his arm around her shoulder, pulling her into him. She immediately felt better. Not completely better, but better.

"So, what do you guys want to do? Can I take you to a late lunch?"

Cole looked down at Lettie, and she shook her head slightly. Then he looked at Ronnie. "No, thanks. We've actually got plans."

Ronnie glared at Lettie. "What? You think you're too good for me?" He looked at Cole. "You want to know the truth about this woman? The kind of white trash she comes from? I could tell you some stories. I could tell *everyone* some stories—"

"Excuse me," Cole interrupted, "your threats don't scare me. And if you tell anyone anything that isn't true, my lawyers will crush you. So, we're going to go now. Don't follow us. Don't contact us again. If Lettie wants to get in touch with you, she will. If you harass her anymore, we'll take legal action to protect her from you." He leaned toward Ronnie just slightly. "Are we clear?"

Ronnie looked speechless. Then he swore. Then he began to mumble, "All high and mighty threatening me, I'll show you ..."

But Lettie didn't hear the rest of what he said, as Cole gently tugged her toward the road, and Ronnie didn't follow. They walked a ways in silence, but Lettie could feel the tension rolling off Cole in waves.

"I'm so sorry," she said.

His eyes widened. "You're sorry? You don't have anything to be sorry for! But I do think we should go back and let everyone know about this development. Mind if I take a rain check on the tattoo?"

If she didn't know better, she might think he sounded relieved. "Of course not. And thank you, Cole."

He shrugged. "I didn't do anything, really."

But he had done something. He'd stuck up for her. He'd cared. He'd been strong.

He waved at a cab, and it slowed to a stop. The driver rolled down the passenger side window and asked if they'd called from the Hostess plant.

"That's us," Cole said and opened the door for Lettie.

She slid into the car and as Cole slid in beside her, she took his hand in hers, and they drove away from the man named Ronnie, who suddenly seemed like no threat at all.

41

Cole's blood was boiling. That guy was such a creep. There was no way he was related to Lettie. He looked *nothing* like her. He almost wished the guy *would* harass them further so he could get him into real trouble.

"You okay?" Lettie asked.

"Oh, yeah, absolutely. Just irritated with that guy." He looked down into her big brown eyes. "Are *you* okay?"

She nodded, but it wasn't convincing. "What if he really is my father?"

"He's not."

"But what if he is?"

"Well, it's pretty easy to find out. No need to make any decisions without knowing." Cole had another thought. "But let's say that he is. Then, so what? Would you really want to do anything about it? And if not, then why bother finding out? Might as well just assume he isn't your father. Which he isn't."

She giggled. "Yeah, you're probably right."

He felt guilty for pressuring her and squeezed her hand. "Sorry, it's not up to me. You take your time and decide what you want to do, and then I will support you no matter what you decide, okay? I just don't like the guy."

"Understandable."

She's always so understanding, he thought. Nothing ever really rattled her. Most women would be far more upset right now, but Lettie just took life in stride. He wanted to tell her. He wanted to confess his love right then and there. He didn't need a tattoo or a song or a dozen black roses or any other grand gesture. He just needed words. He opened his mouth to deliver them when his phone rang.

It was Shawn.

He clamped his mouth shut and pressed the green button on the screen. "Hello?"

"Hi, Cole. Are you on your way back?"

"Yep."

"Good. There are police here waiting to see you. Someone claims you just assaulted them in the Hostess Factory parking lot." Shawn couldn't have sounded more incredulous.

"That's ridiculous!" Cole spouted. "It's the guy Lettie came to warn us about, and I didn't lay a finger on him!" Cole's brain was racing. He didn't know if he'd ever been so indignant.

"I'm sure, but just get back here so we can settle it."

"Tell them to call the factory. I bet they have security footage." Then he hung up the phone without another word.

Lettie's eyes were shiny with tears. "What?"

He leaned over and kissed her on the temple, his lips just barely brushing her skin. "Don't worry. He's saying I assaulted him, but Shawn will work it out."

She looked contemplative. "Do you even have a lawyer?"

"Not yet." He chuckled. "Probably about time I got one, though, huh?"

He still wanted to tell her, but knew it was not a good time. They only had one more show after tonight, in Vegas, and then he was flying home to Nashville for his album launch party. He desperately needed to know where they stood by then, because he wanted to take Lettie as his date.

A long ten minutes later, the taxi pulled into the arena's parking lot, where Branch's buses were all lined up. Maggie stood in front of her bus, all alone, watching his cab approach. She obviously didn't want to be left out of any drama. He looked around, but didn't see any cops.

The door to his bus opened, and Shawn stepped off and headed toward their car. Cole paid the driver and stepped out. Shawn wore a huge smile that Cole found inappropriate for the circumstances.

"What's so funny?" Cole didn't think any of this was funny.

"You were right. There was security footage. The police went to take a look at it, but security at the factory said it clearly shows you walking away and then that lunatic banging his head into a light pole." Shawn laughed.

Cole didn't know whether to join him. It showed *what?* "Seriously?"

Shawn nodded vigorously. "That's what they said." He looked at Lettie, who had just come alongside Cole, and his smile vanished. Cole appreciated this gesture of respect. "There's nothing to worry about, for either of you. We'll make sure the truth is on the six o'clock news, leaving the locals to wonder which one of you is obsessed with Twinkies." He winked at Cole and then started to walk away. "Get ready for your show, Cole. It's going to be a good one!"

Cole looked at Lettie. "Did you hear what he said?"

She shook her head. "No, what?"

Cole searched for tactful words. "Apparently, Ronnie banged his own head into a light post to make it look like he'd been assaulted."

At first, Lettie's face was deadpan, but then a smile quirked up one corner of her mouth, and then the other, and then a giggle escaped, and then another. And then suddenly, she was laughing so hard she had to bend over and put her hands on her knees. Her laughter was contagious, and Cole began to laugh too. Together, they laughed till they cried, and Cole thought his heart might burst with joy and affection for the pink-haired woman who hated music.

He had to tell her. Soon.

42

Lettie woke up in her small bunk, which reminded her of a coffin. This was, of course, okay with her. She had nothing against coffins. She shook the last bit of dream cobwebs out of her head. She had dreamed about the Indianapolis show. She had actually stayed to watch it, now that she was officially on the payroll. It was difficult to take security measures from the tour bus. So she'd watched it from the wings, and then she'd watched it again in her dreams. Perfect. No such thing as too much twang in one night.

The bus was noisy, letting her know that everyone else was awake and moving about. She fumbled for her phone, found it, and was embarrassed to see that she had slept past nine. The rain pounded on the roof of the bus, creating a beautiful, soothing sound that made her want to stay in bed. But—nature called.

She pushed the curtain back and peeked out, immediately making eye contact with Cole. She wasn't sure if she was ever going to get used to seeing him first thing in the morning, before she'd even seen a toothbrush or a hairbrush. She grabbed both and slid out of her bunk to scurry to the tiny restroom, which, blessedly, was vacant.

Just as she stuck her toothbrush in her mouth, the bus lurched to a stop, and she fell into the restroom wall. She grunted and pushed herself back up. It wasn't the first time that had happened, and she wished she could learn to be less annoyed by it. This was her first tour bus. Her mother had always used a broken down van. She'd never been thrown into a wall trying to brush her teeth in that thing.

Someone pounded on the bathroom door. Annoyed, she slid it open, her toothbrush still in her mouth.

It was Cole, all bright-eyed and bushy-tailed.

"How much coffee have you had?" she asked, irritably.

"None. Wanna go for a walk?"

Why was he so jittery? "A walk? In the rain? Where are we?"

"Dunno, somewhere between Indianapolis and Vegas."

No kidding. "I know that, but why did we stop? *Where* did we stop?"

"At a convenience store." He bounced from one foot to the other.

"Why? You obviously don't need more coffee."

"Will you stop about the coffee? Come on, let's go!"

So, without brushing her hair, she followed him down the narrow aisle, wiping toothpaste on her sleeve as she went. Everyone stared at them as they went by. No one else was getting off the bus. Why would they? It was raining out. She looked out the window to see a gas station. "Cole, why did you want to stop here?"

He didn't answer her.

She followed him off the bus.

He turned to look at her. "I asked them to stop here, so I could talk to you. Alone. But hang on. I've got to run inside first. Come on." He took her by the hand, and they ran through the rain toward the front door. For the first time, she envied his wide-brimmed hat. He let go of her to go inside.

"Can't I go in too?"

He shook his head, and rain flew off his hat. "No, but I'll be right back?"

What on earth? The man had truly lost his mind. She stood there under the canopy, but the rain still pelted her from the side. She was beyond irritated. He'd stopped the bus at a deserted gas station in the middle of nowhere to force her to go out into the rain with him and then *not* let her go into the store? This was madness. She turned to push the door open when she met him coming back out. *That was fast.*

"Told you I'd only be a second." He held something behind his back.

For one lunatic second, she thought it might be a diamond ring. Hadn't she seen a rainy gas station proposal in a movie once? *Don't be ridiculous, Lettie, he's not going to propose,* she told herself. No one sells rings at a gas station. Then another lunatic idea boxed the first one out. It was a gun. Did gas stations sell guns? He was going to rob the place. Nah, that didn't make sense either. He didn't have a very inconspicuous getaway vehicle. "What?" she snapped. "What is it? I want to get back on the bus. I'm cold."

"I'm sorry, Lettie, but I have to tell you something, and it can't wait another single second." He pulled his hand out from behind his back to reveal a Ho Ho. "I was going to tell you this at the factory, but we got interrupted."

That's one way to put it.

He handed her the snack and then took off his hat and held it over his chest. "If I don't tell you, I think I might burst. Loretta Jameson, I'm in love with you. I know we are so different, but I don't care. I don't care if you love my music. I just want you to love me. In fact"—he gulped—"if you want me to give it all up, I will. I'd rather have you."

What?! She had no idea what to say, so she just stood there open-mouthed. "Give what up?" she finally managed.

His face fell.

That obviously wasn't what she was supposed to say. "I love you too," she blurted out. Wait. Did she? Did she really love Cole Washburne? Was that even possible? Yes, yes, it was more than possible. It was unavoidable, and she wondered how she'd gone so long without admitting it. She flung her arms around his neck and squeezed, nuzzling her lips against his warm skin that smelled like cedar. She'd never felt anything so perfect in her life.

Then his words came back to her, and she let go abruptly, returned to the ground, and looked up at him. "You don't have to give up anything for me. I would never ask you to give up your career or your dream. Are you nuts?"

He smiled down at her. "I appreciate you saying that. But I needed you to know that I would do that. For you. I know you hate music, and I—"

"I don't hate music, not anymore."

His whole body relaxed, and he put his arms around her waist and pulled her close.

"I still don't love it like a religion," she whispered into his ear, "but it's not fair of me to blame all of music for the things I've been through."

He kissed her then, long and firmly, as if he couldn't get enough. She couldn't get enough either, and only the realization that a busload of people were watching made her pull away from him. "We should get back on the bus," she said softly.

"Okay." He squeezed her hands, gave her another quick kiss, and said, "Thanks for being you, Lettie. You make me a happy man."

She'd never heard sweeter words. "You should put that in a song," she said and then took his hand and led him back to his bus. Back to *their* bus.

Epilogue

Maggie Hammer watched Cole step out onto the stage to headline his first show. She was no longer touring with him, but she'd wanted to support him on this big night, so she stood in the shadows of stage right. She was happy for him, she really was, but she couldn't wait until she was the one headlining.

Only ten feet away stood Cole's fiancée, Lettie, beaming with pride as she watched her man strut around on stage. She wasn't just Cole's fiancée, though; she was also head of his security, which Maggie found a little ridiculous. Little Lettie bossing two burly dudes around.

Maggie returned her eyes to Cole, who was belting out his newest single. The female fans sure were going nuts. Cole knew what he was doing. He finished his song and then put the microphone on its stand so he could slide his guitar strap on over his head. "I'd like to sing a new one for you now. I wrote it for my fiancée, Lettie." He turned and winked at her. Then he turned back to the microphone. "I had to beg, but she gave me permission to sing it for you all tonight. So here goes."

Cole started to sing, and Maggie snuck a look at Lettie. She'd never seen a woman look so happy, so content. For just a second, she was jealous of more than Cole's headlining, but that envy soon faded. If there was such a thing as true love, Maggie didn't have time for it. She had a career to build.

More Books by Penelope Spark

The Diva's Bodyguard (Maggie Hammer's Story)
The Songwriter's Rival (Hannah Carter's Story)
The Billionaire's Blizzard (Branch Bronson's Story)
The Billionaire's Chauffeuress
The Billionaire's Secret Shoes
The Billionaire's Cure
The Billionaire's Christmas
Penelope also writes as Robin Merrill.

www.ingramcontent.com/pod-product-compliance
Lightning Source LLC
Chambersburg PA
CBHW022015170626
46808CB00001B/428

9781393099246